Praise for L.A. Witt's
General Misconduct

"Their romance was sweet, each hero is sweet, and if you love reading fun and adorable heroes falling for each other, it's the perfect getaway book."

~ *USA TODAY*

"...fans of L.A. Witt and military men should check it out. Oh, and those of you who really enjoy virgin heroes that have great first times with a caring partner."

~ *Joyfully Jay*

"I was impressed at the relationship these two young men developed and was rooting for them the whole way."

~ *Rainbow Book Reviews*

"They are such a cute couple and it was a pleasure to watch them go from just hanging out to falling in love."

~ *Love Bytes*

"What a solid, sweet romance this story was! [...] The writing is well done and everything I've come to expect from Ms. Witt."

~ *The Blogger Girls*

Look for these titles by
L.A. Witt

Now Available:

Nine-tenths of the Law
A.J.'s Angel
Out of Focus
Conduct Unbecoming
General Misconduct
The Walls of Troy
Kneel, Mr. President

Tooth & Claw
The Given & the Taken
The Healing & the Dying
The United & the Divided

Writing with Cat Grant
The Only One
The Only One Who Knows
The Only One Who Matters

The Distance Between Us
The Distance Between Us
The Closer You Get
Meet Me in the Middle
Writing with
Aleksandr Voinov
No Distance Left to Run
No Place That Far

As Lauren Gallagher:

Who's Your Daddy?
All the King's Horses
The Princess and the Porn Star
I'll Show You Mine
The Saint's Wife
Not Safe for Work

General Misconduct

L.A. Witt

SAMHAIN
PUBLISHING

Samhain Publishing, Ltd.
11821 Mason Montgomery Road, 4B
Cincinnati, OH 45249
www.samhainpublishing.com

General Misconduct
Copyright © 2014 by L.A. Witt
Print ISBN: 978-1-61922-602-9
Digital ISBN: 978-1-61922-040-9

Editing by Linda Ingmanson
Cover by Angela Waters

First Samhain Publishing, Ltd. electronic publication: July 2014
First Samhain Publishing, Ltd. print publication: July 2015

Chapter One
Aiden

"Go hike to Hiji Falls this weekend," MA1 Randall had said in the emergency room on Friday night. "Take some pictures. Post them on Facebook. Make a few offhand comments about the rocks being slick, and you fell and busted your ass."

"Or my face?" I'd asked dryly.

He'd shrugged. "The rocks are slick, and it's steep. Trust me, it can be done."

I hadn't gone anywhere on Saturday. Partly sleeping off the long night, partly not wanting to venture outside the safety of my apartment. This morning, though, I decided I should put Randall's advice to good use before I went back to work tomorrow.

Parked in front of the half-translated sign at the trailhead, I glanced at myself in the rearview. The bandage over my eyebrow and the welt on my cheekbone glared back. From this angle, I couldn't see the mark on my throat, but it throbbed enough to keep me aware of it. Every time I moved my hand, the raw skin on my knuckles burned. Skepticism swelled in my gut. Would anyone really buy that all this shit had happened in anything less than a fight?

Hopefully, they would. And if my dignity had to take a hit so my career didn't end before it had begun, then so be it.

I sighed and got out of my car.

Though it was still early in the day, the Okinawan heat and humidity were already in full swing. Seemed like a good day to hit the beach and maybe try my hand at snorkeling instead of hiking, but the stitches above my eyebrow begged to differ.

"Keep it clean and dry," the doc had emphatically said before discharging me.

Hiking it was.

Technically, I didn't have to go to Hiji Falls. There were any number of places around the island where I could spend the day and then post on Facebook that I'd busted my ass on some rocks.

But I was rattled and didn't have it in me to think of some other destination besides the one the cop had recommended. That, and I was still terrified of someone finding out what had really happened, and on some irrational level, I'd convinced myself that following his instructions to the letter would keep my secret on the down-low where it belonged. Trust the Naval Academy to beat *that* into my skull.

I started up the trail. I'd heard the kilometer-long hike to Hiji was a steep one, and it lived up to legend. The short stretch from the parking area to the trailhead was good and flat, but then it inclined sharply as it led into the thick forest.

I barely noticed the scenery. My legs burned as I followed the shady trail—and endless staircases—up and down steep slopes and around sharp bends and switchbacks, but my mind was a million miles away.

Friday night shouldn't have happened the way it did. The warning signs had been there from the get-go. Glenn was drunk and so was I, but I'd been coherent. He'd been a little too pushy, a little too in my space, and no amount of haven't-been-laid-in-too-damned-long should have blinded me to those red flags.

Idiot that I was, I'd left Palace Habu with him, and that was when things had gone downhill.

"Why don't we grab a cab and go back to my place?"

"Uh, actually I'd— Let go of my arm."

"Let's go."

"Let's not."

Fifteen minutes later, I was in the back of a cab on my way to the hospital at Camp Lester with a handful of cocktail napkins pressed against the cut above my eyebrow that would *not* stop bleeding. Freaked out. Rattled. Mind full of all the things that could have happened to me if I hadn't landed that punch just right, if I hadn't managed to knock him back long enough to get up and bolt for the end of the alley.

Today, that panic lingered beneath my skin, and God knew I'd spent all of yesterday and last night obsessing over every way things could have happened, scaring myself shitless with all kinds of possibilities, but as I walked down the narrow path toward Hiji Falls, the fear was mostly gone. Now I was angry. Fucking furious.

Not just at Glenn, but at myself.

I was a goddamned second-degree black belt. I had titles in kickboxing and jiu-jitsu. Gold fucking medals, and not just at local competitions. I didn't *get* my ass handed to me.

Grinding my teeth, I stuffed my hands into the pockets of my shorts, brushing my raw knuckles on the seam. I walked faster, as if I could march the fear and anger right out of myself.

My dad had put me in martial arts when I was a kid. The minute he suspected I was gay, he'd enrolled me in every form of self-defense imaginable because he'd been scared to death someone would try to beat me up when they found out. Whether or not it had been necessary was debatable. All I knew was the first time someone took a swing at me, I was fourteen, and no one who heard about that incident ever tried anything after that, no matter how they felt about gays.

And then the first time someone *really* threatened me, someone who intended to do God only knew what once he overpowered me, I'd just barely gotten away from him.

How fucking ironic. My dad had made sure I was extensively trained so I could protect myself from homophobes, and the one who finally bloodied my knuckles and split my eyebrow was another damned gay man.

A chill beneath my skin made me shudder, and I broke out in goose bumps in spite of the heat. Continuing down a flat, winding stretch of trail, I alternated between being on the verge of tears—from shame *and* fear—and wanting to punch something. My pride was as busted up as my face and my hand, but it wasn't just that. The guy scared me. He did. I couldn't pretend he didn't. I'd had training, but so had he. Even the cockiest black belt doesn't take his own skills for granted against a Marine, and even drunk, that Marine had gotten me flat on my back on the pavement.

All the way up the trail, as it rose and fell and took me deeper into the forest, I couldn't stop thinking about what might have happened the other night. What all too easily *could* have happened.

And then what? Was I really going to broadcast to everyone in my chain of command that I'd been in a gay bar on Gate Two Street? Everybody knew the clubs on Gate Two Street could be sketchy, especially the ones down back alleys.

Even if we hadn't met in one of those clubs, I suspected Glenn had the upper hand if our chains of command got involved. He had had just enough lines on his face and gray in his buzz cut to suggest he had a good fifteen years or more on me. Older men were fine and good, but an older American man on this island meant he was stationed here, which meant if he was an officer, he outranked the shit out of me. Even if he was enlisted, he'd have almost an entire career's worth of credibility over an ensign straight out of the academy. Yeah, maybe I could take his career down with allegations of assault—sexual or otherwise—but that didn't mean mine wouldn't go down with his.

I shook my head and kept walking.

Up ahead, a laminated piece of white paper nailed to a post caught my eye. It was in English, so I stopped to read it.

Call Point: This is the place where the electric wave of the mobile phone reaches.

I pulled out my cell phone. Sure enough, I had a few bars. From here on out, I guessed, that wouldn't be the case.

Eyeing the trail ahead of me, I couldn't help feeling a little nervous about moving out into a cell phone dead zone. Glenn was probably sleeping off a hangover somewhere, maybe icing his lip or something, but part of me was sure that the second I lost my ability to call for help, he'd be right there waiting for me around the next bend.

Aiden. For Christ's sake. Just keep going.

I closed my eyes. My sensei had taught me a dozen ways to center myself, to calm myself, and I applied them one after the other. Breathing. Concentrating.

When I opened my eyes again, Glenn was still lurking in the shadows, but the irrational panic was under control. I rolled my shoulders a few times and continued past the sign.

In an effort to ignore Glenn, I tried to concentrate on the scenery. To my surprise, I started to relax a little. It was hard to stay tense and stressed in an environment like this once I actually let myself take it all in. Though the tropical sun was brutal today, the thick canopy of branches and leaves kept the trail comfortably shaded. Beside the trail, a narrow creek wound lazily between trees and boulders, which added a nice backdrop to all the birds singing—or shrieking, in some cases— above me.

The narrow trail had been painstakingly kept, the edges manicured and the staircases well-repaired, which was a nice switch from some of the places I'd hiked back in the States. Nothing wrecked a great hike like twisting an ankle on a rotted step. Though I supposed it would add some credibility to my cover story.

A few other hikers passed me on their way back down. Not a single American among them, but I supposed that wasn't a surprise. Commander Connelly and some of the other guys in the office had mentioned that Americans weren't prone to leaving the bases. I couldn't imagine why anyone would want to stay on base all the time. If I wanted to be contained in a small area, I'd have requested orders to a damned ship.

The falls were close. The deep creek beside the trail ran faster and with more force, and the distinctive sound of crashing, rushing water was louder with every bend in the trail. The closer I got to the falls, the more aware I was of the sweat and humidity dampening my skin and the fierce heat gnawing on the back of my neck. A dozen signs at the beginning of the trail had warned against swimming up here, but I was pretty sure I could be forgiven for bending—okay, breaking—a few rules when it was this hot.

At the very least, I was taking off my boots and putting my feet in the water. Just the thought of that made me feel cooler all over. Whether my cover story ended up holding water—so to speak—or not, this hike had been a damned good idea. I felt better. A lot better. Glenn wasn't here, I wasn't in any danger, and this environment had shaken some of the stress out of me, replacing the tension with a satisfying ache of muscles having to work.

The trail went up again, and then started down, and there were the falls. Gorgeous white water spilled over moss-covered rocks and into a wide pool.

And that was when I saw the most gorgeous set of shirtless shoulders I'd ever seen.

The guy was swimming on the other side of a *No Swimming* sign. Well, not really swimming. More like wading. In the water, anyway, in spite of the emphatic cartoon characters warning of snakes, slick rocks, falling stones and whatever other dangers lurked up here.

His back was to me, which gave me the most jaw-dropping view of those broad, wet shoulders. His soaked black shorts held on to his hips and ass *just* right. Tall, lanky—no way in hell he was much older than me.

He straightened a little and slowly turned around.

Oh. My God.

Definitely not older than me. Probably a few years younger, actually. Twenty, twenty-one tops. Even from here, as I came down the trail on legs that were suddenly not terribly steady, his blue eyes were...disarming.

As far as I could tell, he was American—definitely not Japanese—but there was no way he was military. Not unless he was at least a couple of weeks into some extended leave. His dark hair was too long, the ends curling at the base of his neck.

I stopped at the end of the trail, standing between a couple of rocks near the fence at the edge of the pool. He was maybe ten feet away now, close enough I could see droplets of water sliding down the grooves in his lean, smooth muscles. There was a little bit of dark hair plastered against his chest and his tanned arms, but not a lot.

And he was looking right back at me, eyes locked on mine.

"Hi." I smiled, hoping he'd buy that it was the heat and the hike that had turned my cheeks as red as I was sure they were.

"Hi." He returned the smile. "Another brave one bests the trail and the snakes and makes it to the top."

I laughed. "I didn't see any snakes. Did you?"

"Not this time." His lips quirked. "Were you watching the ground?"

"Where else would I look?"

He gestured above my head. "They hang out in the trees during the day."

Slowly, I lifted my gaze. There weren't any low-hanging branches right here, thank God, but I realized the trail had been shaded almost the entire way. And here I'd been worried about a drunk Marine jumping out at me. "Oh. Awesome. Glad someone mentioned that."

Laughing, the guy in the water waded closer. "Just messing with you. They do hang in the trees, but I've been up here a million times and never seen one."

"You ever seen one at all?"

"Sure." He shrugged. "You do enough hiking, you're going to sooner or later. But as long as they're coiled up in the trees, you're fine. They come at you in the grass, they'll ruin your day."

"So, watching the ground...*is* a good idea?"

"Always. But, you know, keep an eye on the trees." He rested his hip against a boulder. "Nice hike, isn't it?"

Truth be told, I don't remember.

"It's a nice trail." I glanced back at the visible twist of rocks and stairs. "I've definitely hiked worse."

"Recently?" He arched an eyebrow.

"What do you mean?"

He gestured at his face, and I was suddenly hyperaware of the bandages and marks on my face. More heat rushed into my cheeks, and I dropped my gaze. "Oh. That."

"Sorry," he said quietly. "I...didn't realize it..."

"Don't worry about it." I waved a hand and looked him in the eye. "It's a long story."

Awkward silence in three...two...

"You going to get in the water?" He motioned at the enticing pool.

"I, um..." I glanced at the *No Swimming or Wading* sign.

"Don't worry about that." He gestured dismissively. "Seriously, nobody cares."

It wasn't that I was worried about the sign and anyone who might happen along to enforce it. I'd already planned on getting in the water anyway. I just hadn't banked on getting into the same water as someone who was making my legs shake worse than the hilly kilometer I'd just hiked.

Just get in the water, idiot.

I untied the laces and slipped off my boots. Then I emptied my pockets, leaving my car keys and wallet inside one of my boots. I started to pull off my shirt but hesitated. Though the trail was shaded, there was plenty of sunlight up here, and I'd forgotten to pack any sunscreen.

So I left my shirt on. I lifted one of the ropes, ducked under it, and stepped into the water.

And immediately pulled my foot back. "*Shit.*"

He laughed. "Cold?"

"Just a bit." I tried again, dipping my toe in. Then my whole foot. A little at a time, I eased into the water, and by the time I was in up to my knees, I'd adapted to the cold. After the hike to get up here, it felt great.

After I'd waded a little deeper, I scooped some water into my hands, ignoring the way my raw knuckles burned, and leaned down to pour it over the back of my neck. As much as I wanted to splash it on my face, the doc had been pretty emphatic about keeping the stitches clean and dry. Given the microbes that could be lurking in river water...

Though I'd probably already invited those in via the cuts on my knuckles, but whatever.

I turned toward him. "Man, my legs are tired already. You wouldn't think that hike would be that tough. It's not even a mile."

"Except it's all up and down, up and down." He made a gesture like a roller coaster. "We should all be *glad* it's not even a mile."

I laughed. "No kidding." Legs still in the water, I sat on one of the rocks and looked up at the falls. "Wow, this really is amazing."

"It is." He turned to me. "This your first time up here?"

I nodded. "I haven't been on the island long."

"Really?"

"Yep. Just transferred here recently. How long have you been here? On Okinawa, I mean. Not"—I gestured at the falls—"here."

"A few years." He extended his hand. "Name's Connor, by the way."

"Aiden."

His hand was cool and damp from the water, but still hot from his body heat. As we shook hands, our eyes met, and they locked, and...fuck. Wow, he really was hot. Especially up close. Those blue eyes were unreal.

I released his hand, and as we both sat back, he gave me the oddest little smile, one that seemed caught somewhere between shy and cocky. Before I could figure out which, he broke eye contact and busied himself leaning over to scoop some water onto his arms. It was hard to tell, but I thought his cheeks might've turned pink.

"So do you come up here a lot?" I asked.

"Every now and then." Connor splashed some more water onto his arms and then leaned back against the rock. "It's one of my favorite places on the island."

"I can see why. Where else do you like to go?"

"You can't really go wrong on this rock. I've been to all the castles, the outlying islands, the good snorkel spots." He shrugged. "Just depends on what you're into, I guess."

"Do you dive?"

"I tried." Connor tapped just below his temple. "It bugs my ears."

"Damn."

"Tell me about it. There's some awesome places to snorkel here. I'll bet diving would be even better."

"Well, I've never even snorkeled."

"Really?"

"Really." I mirrored his earlier motions, leaning down and scooping some water—holy *fuck*, that stung my knuckles—onto my arms to cool myself off. "Any good spots?"

"I haven't found a bad spot here. Though I did stop snorkeling off Kadena Marina after I realized it's right next to a sewage treatment plant."

I wrinkled my nose. "Seriously?"

He nodded. "I don't know if they actually dump anything in the water, and it all looks pretty clean and clear, but...no way I'm putting my face in that water."

"I don't blame you."

"Other than that, though, you can pretty much pull off the road anywhere, jump in the water, and see all kinds of cool shit. Just, you know, watch for jellyfish."

"That's what I've heard." I sat back against the rock and, without thinking about it, propped my foot up on the other rock...just inches from his leg.

He glanced down, and that odd smile came back to life as he looked at me again. There was no casually pulling my leg back and pretending it had never happened, so I just kept it against the rock.

Clearing my throat, I broke eye contact. "You had any problems with jellyfish when you've snorkeled?"

"Not the box jellyfish. Never even seen one, knock on wood."

I lifted my gaze. "Are there others?"

Connor nodded. "Buddy of mine got stung in the face by one of the red ones. Those fuckers won't kill you, but, man, they will ruin your day."

"Yeah?"

"Yep. Watch out for them. They're red and about this big." He held his hands up about a football's width apart. "Nasty fuckers."

"Good to know."

Silence fell between us. My foot was still on the rock next to him. He was still fucking with my pulse just by existing. I had no idea if he was gay, straight or just a goddamned figment of my sex-deprived imagination, and what to say next was completely lost on me.

Fortunately, Connor spoke first. "Listen, um..." He paused, gnawing his lower lip. "There's a place not far from here, maybe an hour once you get back to the main drag. Some of the most amazing pizza on the island. You, um, want to grab a bite?"

In spite of this unbelievable attraction, my first instinct was to back away and quickly decline, but this wasn't some drunk Marine trying to coax me into a dark corner. Connor was as nonthreatening as a man could be. And so, *so* gorgeous.

I smiled. "Sure. Why not?"

Chapter Two
Connor

I always took my time on the way back down from Hiji Falls. For one thing, the heat made sure my shorts were dry by the time I made it to my car. Mostly, though, it was the scenery. It was green year-round—not quite a jungle, according to my high school biology teacher, but close. Every time I made this hike, I found something unusual, whether it was an odd plant I'd never seen before or some insect or lizard.

Today? I took my sweet time, but it wasn't because of the scenery.

In some places, the trail was too narrow to walk side by side. I didn't mind—especially when Aiden went ahead—but in others there was room for both of us as long as we were okay with occasionally brushing sleeves or arms. Again, I didn't mind.

It was just as well we were walking so slowly. Some of the stairs up here, especially near the falls, were steep, uneven and just asking for a guy to fall and bust his ass. Especially when that guy was too preoccupied to pay attention to where he was putting his feet.

And, holy crap, was I preoccupied.

I was used to hot men on this island. I'd nearly killed myself probably a dozen times because of shirtless, tattooed Marines jogging along the roadside, and whenever I went to the gym on base, it wasn't my workout that jacked up my heart rate. Gorgeous, fit men were just part of living here.

But Aiden. *Fuck.*

I was thankful I'd been waist-deep in cold water when I'd first laid eyes on him. Pretty boys weren't usually my type, but the bruise and bandage on his face gave him an edge that made my knees weak. Judging by the scrapes on his knuckles, he'd given as good as he'd gotten, and... What could I say? He was hot. Pretty boy or not, even if he *hadn't* had the battle scars, he sure was easy on the eyes.

Military too. Okay, so almost every American guy on Okinawa was military, but with some it was more obvious than others. At least he wasn't one of those dudes who walked around like he had a stick up his ass. You could always tell the ones who were fresh out of boot camp—it was like they couldn't stop themselves from constantly being at attention. Aiden stood straight, but he wasn't that bad.

He was blond, and his hair was still within regs, but just long enough for the humidity, sweat and water to muss it up. I wondered what he looked like with his hair all combed and perfect. That had to be hot. Or in his uniform? Jesus. I didn't ask what branch he was in—the less I knew about him, the less he needed to know about me—but he must've been Air Force or Navy. Marines were never this relaxed. And if he was by chance a Marine, God help the guy who'd fucked up his face.

At the top of one of the staircases, Aiden stopped and exhaled. "Man, I'm not in bad shape, but this has got to be the longest kilometer on this entire island."

I laughed. "Yeah. And the humidity doesn't help."

He shook his head. "No, it doesn't. I'm starting to think I need to spend more time at the gym, though."

Oh God. An image flickered through my mind of Aiden sweating on a treadmill or lifting weights, and suddenly the tropical weather had nothing to do with my rising body temperature.

I cleared my throat. "You think this is a hell of a hike, you should go up to the mainland and hike Fuji one of these days."

"Yeah?" He wiped some sweat off his forehead, wincing as he brushed the bandage above his eye. "Have you been up there?"

I held up two fingers. "Well, technically three times, but I had to turn back the second time."

"Wore yourself out?"

"Bad weather. Happens up there sometimes."

"Ouch. That sucks."

"Yeah, just a—" Movement caught my eye. I turned, and a lizard stared back at me from on top of a rock. It was one of those weird green-and-brown tree lizards that couldn't decide if it wanted to be a gecko or a chameleon.

"Hey." I pointed at it. "Check this out."

Aiden stopped. "What am I looking at?"

"On top of the rock."

"I don't—oh, there it is." He leaned in a little closer, moving slowly enough he didn't startle the critter. "I've never seen one like that."

"They're kind of weird looking, aren't they?"

Aiden nodded.

The lizard watched us for a moment and then skittered up another rock. There it stopped to look back at us again, but a second later it shot into the bushes and disappeared. We both laughed, and I was about to say something, but when I looked at him, he looked right back at me, and I forgot what I was going to say. For a split second, I couldn't even remember what language I spoke. Was it even possible for someone to have eyes that green?

I cleared my throat and gestured at the trail. "I guess we should keep moving."

"Right. Yeah." He made a similar gesture. "We're, what, halfway back?"

"I think so, yeah. I always lose track. Isn't like they mark the trail, you know?" And why the fuck was I rambling like an idiot? Biting my tongue, I continued walking, and he fell into step beside me.

A few steps in, he glanced at me. Then he faced forward, and I took a chance and stole a quick look at him. My heartbeat was all over the place, and it wasn't because of the hike. I could do this hike in my sleep and still have enough left for a run when I got back to the base, but he was tripping me up left, right and center.

I had no idea if Aiden was gay. I'd never had much of the "gaydar" a lot of guys claimed to have. It didn't help that on this island, Americans tended to cluster together even if they met out in town or something. Two guys could run into each other on a beach and spend the whole day talking and hanging out just because they spoke the same language, which made it really fucking complicated for guys like me who could've seriously gone for some kind of code word for *I speak English* and *I'm into dick*.

But with Aiden, I really didn't care if he was gay. I liked talking to him. Yeah, sure, he was some serious eye candy— Jesus Christ, he was gorgeous—but if he turned out to be straight...oh fucking well. Him and every other man on this island. Walking and talking with him was still fun. I didn't even mind walking and *not* talking, which we'd been doing for a little while now since we'd stopped to watch the lizard.

Aiden cleared his throat. "So, are there any other places like this on the island? Hiking spots, I mean?"

"Oh yeah. They're all over the place."

"Yeah?"

I nodded. "You have got to check out Nakijin Castle..."

The last steep slope of the trail leveled out and led us past the picnic area at the bottom. As the parking lot came into view, I said, "It's a bit of a drive from here, so it's probably best if you just follow me."

"Cool. I'm parked right over there." He gestured at the other end of the short lot, where a piece-of-shit silver Toyota sat in the shade.

"Mine's over here." I nodded toward where my equally shitty brown Nissan was parked and then pulled my cell phone out of my backpack. "The route gets a little tricky once we're off 329, so I'll give you my number in case we get separated."

Aiden took out his cell, and we put our contact information into each other's phones. He spelled his out—Aiden Lange—but I just put in my first name. Aiden was obviously military, and I wasn't quite ready for him to figure out who my dad was and run screaming for the hills. That time would probably come, but...not today.

"Okay, so we've got a backup in case we get separated." He slid his phone back into his pocket. "Assuming there's a signal."

I laughed. "Yeah, good luck with that. Best bet is to *not* get separated."

"I'll be right behind you."

We exchanged a long—*holy fuck, he's gorgeous*—look and then retreated to our cars. Mine was hot from being out here most of the day, so I rolled down the windows and blasted the AC. While the car cooled down, I backed out of the spot and started out of the parking lot, but stopped to let Aiden catch up with me.

One glance in the rearview, and... Yeah, the windows and AC didn't help. At all.

Get a grip, Connor.

Yeah, right.

All the way to the pizza place, with Aiden's car in my rearview, I still couldn't get my pulse to settle down. I was used to hot men as far as the eye could see, but I wasn't used to them giving me the time of day. Or giving me those little looks that could've been read as innocent glances or something that wasn't even in the same ballpark as innocent.

And I definitely wasn't used to them taking me up on an offer to jump in the car and go grab a bite to eat.

But there he was.

Forty-five minutes or so after we'd left Hiji, I turned into the unmarked, unpaved parking area outside a nondescript house. My heart started beating faster as Aiden pulled his car up beside mine.

He got out of his car and looked around, brow furrowed. "This is the place?"

I gestured at the tile roof sticking out from between the trees. "Yep. Doesn't look like much, but I think you'll like it."

"Lead the way."

We walked up the path to the house, which was actually the restaurant, and a hostess invited us in. We took off our shoes and then followed her to a table.

This place was out in the middle of nowhere, up on top of a hill overlooking the East China Sea. Wasn't the greatest place in the world to eat after a long hike—sitting on the floor hurt like hell—but the food made it worthwhile.

"This is easily the best pizza on the island," I said as we settled in cross-legged on the tatami mats beside the low wooden tables.

"Yeah?" He shifted a bit to get comfortable.

I nodded. "Trust me. There's a reason people are willing to get their dumb asses lost trying to find it."

He chuckled and glanced toward the road. "I can see how people would get lost out here."

"Everyone does. Anyone tells you they found this place on the first try, they're lying through their teeth."

Picking up the menu, he said, "Are they also lying if they say they can read the menu?"

"Most of them? Yes." I waved a hand. "Nobody can read menus on this island unless there's pictures."

He turned it around to show me. "I think they forgot to give us the picture menu."

"It's okay. They only have one kind of pizza anyway."

A waitress came up to us right then, and I ordered us a pizza and a drink for myself. Aiden managed to find something to drink on the menu—Coke, of course—and ordered that. When she returned ten or fifteen minutes later with our food, Aiden eyed the pizza, and I laughed. I couldn't exactly blame him. The pizza here was different, that was for sure. Not quite a flatbread, not quite a hand-tossed crust, and amongst the melted cheese and tiny pepperonis, there was...corn. Weird. But, sweet Jesus, it tasted amazing.

"Try it." I gestured at it. "Trust me."

He threw me a suspicious look but then shrugged and reached for the pizza. The second he touched it, he snatched his hand back. "Fuck! Maybe I should let it cool a bit first."

"Oh yeah. It's hot."

With a playful scowl, he said, "Thanks for letting me know before I burned my hand."

"Sorry," I said with a semi-apologetic shrug.

Aiden rolled his eyes. Then he smiled, though one corner of his mouth didn't rise quite as high, probably thanks to the bruising along the edge. "So it seems like you know this island pretty well."

"I'd better know it. I've been here long enough."

"Is that right?" He tilted his head slightly. "You're not military, though, are you?"

"No." The question lingered in his eyes—curious more than demanding. "I..." Some warmth rushed into my cheeks, and I focused on pulling a slice of steaming-hot pizza onto my plate. "I still live with my parents."

"There's no shame in that," Aiden said. "Especially if you've been here for several years."

"Okay, true. I just hate being that guy who still lives at home when he's twenty."

Something in him seemed to settle.

Yes, I'm legal, I wanted to say, but bit it back.

He tested the pizza again, and it must've cooled a bit because he tore off a piece. "So you must be in college, then?"

I met his eyes and nodded. "Yeah. Thank God for the on-base campus." Cringing inwardly, I waited for the inevitable chain of questions. *So I'm guessing your dad's military? What branch? Yeah? What does he do? No shit? What's his name? Oh fuck.* That's *your dad?*

But the questions didn't come. As he chewed the bite of pizza, Aiden shifted his attention out to our view of the village and the water below us. I subtly watched him and couldn't help glancing at that nasty-looking gash above his eyebrow. There was a thin bandage over it, and the stitches were still visible, sticking out along the edges like the legs of a squashed spider. The bruising on his jaw and cheekbone wasn't serious, but it was still fairly fresh—bluish-purple without the green halo that fading bruises usually had. And whatever he'd done to his raw knuckles? Definitely recent. *Very* recent.

"So, out of curiosity." I gestured at my face as Aiden turned toward me. "What happened? To your, uh..."

"This?" He gestured at the bandaged cut.

I nodded.

His cheeks colored, and he lowered his gaze. "It's a long story." Though he didn't say it, the *and I don't want to tell it* came through loud and clear.

Awkward silence fell.

I was about to break the silence when Aiden cleared his throat and beat me to the punch. "Listen, uh, I'll probably need to get back to the base after we eat. Early morning tomorrow. But, um..." He met my eyes through his lashes. "Do you want to get together again?"

My heart jumped. "Sure. Yeah."

Aiden smiled, and I hadn't realized how tense his neck and shoulders were until they relaxed a bit. "Great. I'm off work tomorrow at four. Since you seem to know the island pretty well, maybe you could show me some other place?"

"Yeah, definitely."

"I'll text you directions to my apartment." He picked up his pizza. "Meet me there at four thirty, five or so?"

"You bet."

Chapter Three
Aiden

Paperwork. I'd been doing something involving...paperwork. It was probably important—at least to whoever was waiting for it, anyway—but hell if I could remember what I was supposed to be doing with it.

Blinking a few times, I tried to make sense of the papers and printed words fanned out on the desk in front of me. I'd been working on them, making progress, and then...not.

I rewound the last few minutes, trying to figure out where things had gone wrong. A few minutes ago, Lieutenant Commander Gonzales had come into the office. She'd given me that stack of folders. Right. Got it.

"My God, Ensign." She'd grimaced. "What in the world happened to you?"

"What happ— Oh, this?" I'd gestured at my face and then shrugged. "Had a graceful moment up at Hiji Falls over the weekend."

Oh.

Right.

That.

She left, and my mind went right back to Hiji Falls, and paperwork? What paperwork?

Sitting back in my chair, I sighed. Hiji Falls. Connor. Friday night had been one of the worst nights of my life, but damn, Sunday had been a switch. The hike had been therapeutic in its own right, giving me a chance to relax and catch my breath and try to make sense of having my ass handed to me two nights prior, but when I'd reached the falls...

I shivered and closed my eyes. Could he have been a little less gorgeous? Maybe not fucked with my blood pressure quite so much?

Oh hell. Who was I kidding? I'd loved it. Every second of it. And I still loved it, because it hadn't ended when we'd gone our separate ways. Even after his taillights had disappeared on the highway and I'd been on my own, flying along the coastline on my way back to the base, I'd been dizzy and distracted and barely kept myself from chasing him down and maybe even working up the nerve to move in for that elusive kiss.

I hadn't, though. I still wasn't even sure if Connor was gay. Not that he could have made it much more obvious. Seriously, what was I waiting for? An engraved invitation? A neon sign saying *I'm gay, I'm attracted, and if you don't kiss me, I'm gone*?

Something told me if I did kiss him, *I'd* be the one who was gone, probably in the form of smoke and ashes. Even Glenn— prior to becoming a colossal douche bag—hadn't been as attractive as Connor, and the more time I spent with Connor, the more I was liable to—

Hey. Lange. Paperwork. Pronto.

I shook my head and looked at the paperwork again.

And of course, my mind drifted right back. To the falls, to the drive, to that pizza we'd shared high above the East China Sea. There was no way in hell I'd ever find that pizza place again. Not without Connor's license plate in front of me the whole way. I didn't even remember what the food tasted like. It was good, that much I remembered, but everything else was a blank.

Everything else, I thought as I tried for the hundredth time to focus on my paperwork. Good God. What the hell was wrong with me? I hadn't been this caught up with someone in ages.

Not since Cadet Williams at the Academy. And even that little fling didn't hold a candle to this. Or maybe it just didn't seem to, since I was comparing something that had faded a year or so ago to something that had only been going for like twenty-four hours and hadn't even gotten off the ground. I might've gotten this giddy and spacey over him. I didn't remember. What was I thinking about again?

Oh.

Right.

Connor.

Again.

I scrubbed a hand over my face and immediately regretted it when my finger rubbed painfully over the stitches above my eye.

My phone rang, startling me out of my thoughts. When I answered, the well-rehearsed greeting came out automatically: "ATO office, this is Ensign Lange. How may I help you, sir or ma'am?"

"Ensign, it's General Bradshaw," came the low, grumbled response. "I need that threat-assessment package for Gates 1 and 3. How are you coming on that?"

I pulled the drab-green folder from my inbox and glanced at it. "It's nearly done, sir. Just needs a signature from Colonel Patterson."

"Drop it by my office before the end of the day."

"Will do, sir."

After we'd hung up, I figured I wasn't going to get much done that required actual concentration, so I might as well start making my daily rounds for signatures, stamps and approval. Along with the threat assessment Bradshaw had asked for, I gathered up the rest of the documents that needed to be approved by various officers and headed out of my office.

First stop, Colonel Patterson's office.

God, please let him be in a decent mood today.

I didn't just work with Navy at this command. Kadena was primarily an Air Force base, and our particular building had everybody. Navy. Air Force. Marines. I thought I saw some Army guys around one day, probably from Torii Station, their base a few clicks up the road. Joint commands didn't bother me. High-ranking officers didn't bother me either—I respected rank but wasn't intimidated by it—which was good, since I worked with captains, colonels, a general and the odd admiral on a daily basis. But some of the *particular* captains, colonels and generals? Jesus, these guys could be assholes.

At the end of the hall, I stopped in front of the colonel's office.

Cringing, I knocked on the door.

"Come in." Terse but not angry. Good. Ever since the man's wife had taken the kids and gone back stateside, he'd been almost as volatile as that asshole Commander Morris. If either of them had been allowed to drink at work, there would have been a fistfight in this building by now.

I stepped into the office. "Good morning, Colonel."

"Ensign," he muttered.

I pulled three folders off the stack tucked under my arm and handed them to him.

Colonel Patterson perused the folders, then tossed them aside and muttered, "Dismissed, Ensign."

"Thank you, sir."

I quickly left his office and continued down the hall, waiting until I was a few doors down before I exhaled. That man was seriously not good for my blood pressure.

Once I'd shrugged Colonel Patterson away, I continued down the hall to the next office. I knocked on General Bradshaw's door, and he gruffly told me to come in.

"Sir," I said with a slight nod. I handed the stack of folders to him over the top of his desk and then stood back and waited to be dismissed.

General Bradshaw scowled as he skimmed over the threat assessment. He was tough to read. Did the scowl mean he'd found something he didn't like? Or was he just focusing on the words? I hoped to God it was the latter. I'd been on the receiving end of a few of his notorious tirades, and now I made *triple* sure all my *i*'s were dotted and my *t*'s were crossed before I put anything in front of him.

Finally, he put the documents aside. "Dismissed, Ensign."

"Thank you, sir." I left his office and continued getting signatures and dispersing documents to those who needed them. Much as the task annoyed me sometimes, it was the most brainless part of my job, and it was welcome today. Something I could accomplish even while I was mentally elsewhere.

On the way back to my office, I passed by Commanders Mays and Morris. Mays gave me a slight nod, but Morris avoided eye contact and did a piss-poor job of hiding the disgust curling his lip. I just waited until we'd passed, and then rolled my eyes. I'd only been here a short while, and I'd already learned to brush off Commander Morris's scowls and glares. Scuttlebutt had gotten around, and I knew what his problem was.

Yeah, yeah, yeah. You've figured out I'm gay, and you don't like queers. Whatever, dude.

I was a few steps past them when Mays said, "Oh hey, Ensign."

I turned around. "Yes, sir?"

"I looked over your Island Indoc PowerPoint, and it looks good, but how about a couple more slides emphasizing the off-limits areas?"

"Sure, I can do that."

"Good. E-mail it to me as soon as you can."

"Yes, sir. Will do."

I waited until he'd dismissed me and I was on my way down the hall before I rolled my eyes. Island Indoc. Awesome. It was the briefing everyone had to endure when they first came to Okinawa, and one of those things that made the word "briefing" hilariously ironic. More like ten hours of my life I was never getting back. There were presentations on things everyone already knew about, like not shoplifting, or drinking and driving, and maybe five minutes of actual valuable shit, like Japanese etiquette and a few necessary phrases.

Fortunately, I only had to show up for my own presentation now, and I tried my damnedest not to bore the crowd out of their skulls. Death by PowerPoint sucked for everyone, myself included. I kept mine as short as possible, but invariably someone—like Commander Mays, in this case—wanted me to add slides. At least he only wanted me to add two. Captain Warren had nearly doubled the length of my last presentation.

I headed back toward my office to dive into PowerPoint and try not to bore myself into a coma. Maybe I could combine the information he wanted onto one slide. It was pretty simple. No reason it *needed* to be on two. I could always—

"Ensign Lange."

I turned around to see Commander Connelly leaning out of his office. "Yes, sir?"

"Would you mind stepping in here for a minute?"

I glanced at the papers in my hand, which I needed to take care of before the end of the day. But when a commander said "jump"...

I followed him into his office.

He closed the door behind us. That was a little disconcerting. He wasn't in my chain of command. I didn't answer to him. There really was no reason I could think of for us to meet behind closed doors.

"Have a seat, Ensign." He gestured at one of the chairs in front of his desk.

With no clue why, I did as I was told, keeping the folders full of signed documents securely in both hands in my lap.

Connelly sat back in his chair. "Looks like you did quite a number on your face."

My cheeks burned. "Just a little mishap up at Hiji Falls."

"I see." His skepticism turned my stomach. No one else had given me any reason to think they didn't believe me, but Commander Connelly didn't seem convinced.

And so what if he wasn't? What did he care?

He leaned forward and folded his arms on the edge of his desk. "This conversation is entirely off the record, Ensign."

I swallowed. Hadn't I heard almost those exact words recently? "Okay..."

"And it's man to man. All this?" He gestured at the insignia on his uniform. "Just ignore it for a minute, okay?"

"Uh..."

"My name's Shane, by the way."

I chewed my lip. "Aiden."

"All right. Aiden." He tilted his head slightly. "Have you ever met an MA1 Randall?"

All the blood slipped out of my face. "I..."

He smiled. "Relax. I'm not interrogating you here, and nothing leaves this room."

"Then maybe you could tell me why we're having this conversation?"

He regarded me silently for a moment. Then, speaking even quieter now, he said, "He's the one who told you to go up to Hiji Falls, isn't he?"

My heart stopped. "What? He said that was confidential, and—" And I just admitted it. Way to go, Lange.

Shane put up a hand. "Relax. He didn't give me details, and he didn't mention your name. He just told me that some ensign came into the ER with"—he gestured at his face—"some cuts and bruises. Said the kid was afraid of being outed."

Outed. Oh fuck.

I chewed my lip but couldn't look at the commander.

"When you came in this morning," he went on, "I put two and two together. Kind of guessed it was you."

I still kept my gaze down and hoped I could keep my lunch down too. Fuck. Fuck, this wasn't—

"Look at me, Ensign." His voice was gentler than I expected.

Cringing inwardly, I lifted my gaze. There was nothing but kindness and empathy in his eyes, but I still couldn't relax. Not when he *knew*.

"Do you want to know why MA1 Randall was talking to me about this in the first place?

Now that you mention it...

I just nodded.

Shane glanced at the door, a subtle but surprising display of nerves. When he met my eyes again, he said, "MA1 Randall is my boyfriend."

"He's..." I blinked a few times. "You're..."

"He is, and I am. The reason he was telling me about you was because he was upset about what happened to you. And the reason I called you in here is that I wanted you to know you're not the only one. I know how rough it is, even these days. I just wanted to let you know that if anyone hassles you, my door is always open."

I didn't even know what to say. "I..."

"How was Hiji Falls, anyway?"

Oh, it was much better than I thought it would be...

"It was nice," I said. "Hell of a hike."

"It is a nice one, isn't it?" Shane said. "Anyway, I just wanted to let you know the door's open, and you're not alone."

I got up. "Thank you, Commander."

"You're welcome. And I mean it. Door's open any time you need it."

"I appreciate it." I reached for the door, opened it, but then paused. After a second, I closed the door again. As I faced Shane, I said, "Just one question."

"Hmm?"

"You said you and Randall are..."

Shane nodded.

"But isn't he..." I gestured at my insignia.

The commander stiffened slightly. "Yes." His eyebrows rose a little, and I thought I heard an unspoken *is my secret safe with you?*

"Oh." I shrugged. "I was just curious."

He didn't relax.

"Not a word," I said. "Promise."

After a second, the tension in his shoulders eased. "Thanks."

I pulled his door closed behind me and exhaled. Maybe the other night with Glenn had a silver lining after all. He'd rattled me, split my eyebrow and bloodied my knuckles, but I'd gained a pair of allies in both MA1 Randall and Commander Connelly.

And I'd stumbled across Connor.

Connor, who I'd see in just a couple of hours.

Smiling to myself, I headed back to my office to count down to four o'clock.

Chapter Four
Connor

Just left the office. Meet you at my place in 20?

I was out of my desk chair and halfway down the hall before I'd even finished reading Aiden's message. On the way down the stairs, I wrote back, *See you then.*

My stepmother, Hitomi, was in the kitchen with my little sister and glanced up as I passed through. "Going out?"

"Yep," I threw over my shoulder. "I'll be out late."

"Have fun." At least she never asked questions. My dad hadn't quite accepted the fact that even though I lived with him, I was an adult. If he'd been here now, he'd have grilled me about the where, when and—most importantly—with whom of my plans for the evening. The joys of still living at home.

But he wasn't due back from work for an hour yet, so I slipped out the front door, got in my car and headed out of housing. Aiden had sent me directions to his place earlier, and I followed those off the base and up the highway.

His apartment was out near White Beach in a small cluster of pastel-colored concrete cubes behind the shopping mall. A pair of foot-tall terra-cotta shi shi dogs flanked the entrance to the tight parking lot, and I squeezed my car in between a souped-up sports car and a minivan, both with Japanese plates. Most of the plates in the lot were Japanese owned, aside from one faded-green Nissan that was American owned.

As I was getting out of my car, a familiar beat-up car pulled in, and my heart skipped when I glimpsed Aiden's face through the windshield. I waved, and he waved back, and I waited while he parked in one of the narrow reserved spots closer to the building.

His engine shuddered and then quieted. My heart beat a little faster, especially as the driver's side door opened. As Aiden stepped out of his car, I tried like hell not to drool. Back at Hiji, I'd suspected he usually kept his hair pristine and perfect, and I was right. The wind was playing with it a little, but it was combed into place like he'd spent hours on it this morning.

And he was Navy, apparently. They were the only ones who had those bright white uniforms, and Aiden was born to wear it. It was like those white pants had been designed specifically for Aiden's ass, and I looked the hell away because my shorts had definitely *not* been designed to accommodate a stealth boner.

He came around behind the car and gave a shy smile, his chin down a bit and his eyebrows pulled together, which seemed really strange when he still had enough scrapes and bruises to look like he'd recently fucked somebody up.

"Hey," he said.

"Hey." I hoped my cheeks weren't too red after I let my gaze briefly—*very* briefly—dart below his shiny belt buckle.

"I, um..." He pointed with his car keys at the building beside us. "I need to grab a shower and put on some civvies. Won't be a minute."

"Sure. No rush."

Another smile, maybe a little shier than the one before, and we headed upstairs. In the breezeway on the second floor, he keyed open the door. I tried not to read too much into his hand being a little shaky. It was still healing, after all, so maybe it hurt to do even simple things like unlocking doors.

Aiden waved me into the apartment, which was nice and cool after being out in the humidity. "I'll just be a minute. Make yourself at home."

"Take your time."

As he disappeared down the hall, I tried not to think about how close I was to his bedroom. I'd been horny as fuck ever since Hiji, and I was really tempted to suggest we explore something *besides* Okinawa tonight, but I didn't. For all I knew, he was straight, maybe even married or with a girlfriend or something. I wasn't great at reading guys. When I thought a guy was gay, he was straight. When I thought he was flirting, he was just talking to pass the time. And when I was absolutely sure the straight guy was talking to me to pass the time, it turned out he was gay and flirting with a capital *F*. I really sucked at being gay.

So for right now, I just bit my tongue and decided I'd see where this evening went.

The shower kicked on in the other room. I rocked back and forth from my heels to the balls of my feet, and checked out my surroundings.

Aiden must not have been here very long. He did say he was new to the island, didn't he? It was obvious now—boxes everywhere, some open, some not. He'd put a few things up on the wall, but it was still pretty bare for the most part. A framed diploma from the Naval Academy at Annapolis was propped up against the wall, so he probably intended to hang it there eventually.

Some framed photos were on top of a box. Looked like Aiden came from a family that must've been still intact—he resembled both his parents way too much for either of the smiling, tanned people in that picture to be a stepparent.

In the other room, the shower stopped. A few minutes later, Aiden came down the hall, dressed in cargo shorts and a plain blue T-shirt with a pair of sturdy sandals—the kind you could wear hiking or climbing all over shit without getting hurt or too hot. His hair was damp, and had been flawlessly arranged again. About the time I caught myself wondering what it would feel like to run my fingers through it, I cleared my throat and gestured at the door.

"Ready to go?"

"Definitely." He spun his keys on his finger. "We never did figure out where we're going, though."

"Well"—*your bedroom sounds like a winner*—"have you ever been up to Cape Hedo?"

Aiden cocked his head. "I've heard about it but never been. What's up there?"

"Cliffs and water. Want to see it?"

"Absolutely. If you'll tell me how to get there, I'll drive."

We left my car at his apartment, and I slid into the passenger seat of Aiden's car. Yesterday, he'd followed me, and I couldn't deny that I got a little thrill out of being in the same car with him now.

And we'd be in here for a while too, which was absolutely deliberate. Cape Hedo really was one of my favorite places on the island, but secretly that wasn't the reason I'd suggested it today. It had more to do with the eighty-nine kilometer drive. On an island this small, it was one of the farthest points away from where we were.

And a longer drive meant more time in the car with Aiden.

Perfect.

At an intersection a few blocks from his apartment, he pointed at a sign for the expressway. "That where I want to go?"

"Yeah. Head north. It won't take us all the way up, but it'll save us some time." Not that I necessarily *wanted* to save time, but I did want to get us there before the sun went down. We could always take the long way back.

Aiden pulled up to the tollbooth and took a ticket. He handed it to me and continued onto the expressway.

"Fair warning." He grinned at me as the engine whined and the painted stripes whipped by faster. "I have a bit of a lead foot."

I laughed and glanced at him. "I won't tell if you won't."

Aiden chuckled, facing forward, and accelerated. The speed limit out here was eighty clicks, which amounted to about fifty-five miles an hour, but nobody paid attention to it.

Especially not Aiden, apparently. He wasn't lying about his lead foot, and as we screamed past other cars in the right lane—the passing lane in this country—I was almost dizzy from the speed. Though I still wanted this drive to take a while, I wasn't about to tell him to slow down. There was something intoxicating about speeding up the expressway with him. The needle on the dash was creeping up on a hundred and twenty, and it felt like that was miles an hour instead of kilometers, like we really were being reckless and dangerous, and I loved it. He might've just been in this for the tour guidance and a little company, but I let myself get lost in being next to him. Because, hell, why not?

Once we got up past Nago and left the expressway, the drive was slower, but the scenery was really pretty. The highway mostly hugged a seawall built along the coast. There were a few small towns—more like villages—along the way, but a lot of it was just open country and forested hills. I came up here by myself all the time, driving all over the place with no destination in mind, and having Aiden next to me made it almost surreal. I could barely believe this place existed, and I could barely believe *he* existed, and now I was experiencing both at the same time. If this weren't real and someone had slipped me some acid or shrooms or something, I hoped like hell they didn't wear off any time soon.

"So you've really never been up here?" I asked as he followed Highway 329 along the coast.

Looking out at the water, Aiden shook his head. "Hiji Falls is the furthest north I've ever been."

I smiled. "Then you're in for a treat. The north end of the island is awesome."

"Is it?"

"Yep. The south end was bombed out pretty bad in World War II, so a lot of the old stuff is gone, but the north end? Old growth and ancient buildings. Wicked cool."

"In that case..." The engine whined as he accelerated.

We talked about random shit as the highway wound along the seawall, mostly shooting the breeze about nothing until something caught his eye.

"What are those things?" He gestured out at some huge structures in the water. They were maybe thirty yards long, built out of what looked like jacks made out of concrete.

"They're tsunami breaks." I watched the surf breaking against the jacks. "When a tsunami comes in, it hits those and breaks up a little before it hits the seawall that we're on right now."

"Brilliant engineering."

"It's Japan. Of course it is."

"Fair point, fair point. So how far to—" His phone buzzed on the dash. Aiden grabbed it and glanced at the caller ID. "Fuck. I need to answer this."

"Better stop so the JPs don't bust you."

"Yeah, I know." He pulled over and picked up the phone. "Ensign Lange." Someone spoke on the other end. "Yes, sir. Right. Yes, sir. Understood. Yes, sir. I'll have it on your desk in the morning, sir."

"Boss?" I asked as he hung up the phone and set it on the dash.

"Yep." Aiden rolled his eyes and then pulled out onto the deserted highway. "It's always something, and it's usually something that can wait until tomorrow."

I laughed. "What do you do, anyway?"

"I'm the command antiterrorism officer." He smirked. "And trust me, it's not nearly as fun as it sounds."

Snickering, I said, "It doesn't sound fun to me at all, actually."

"It's not. It's pretty much paperwork and PowerPoint."

I wrinkled my nose. "I think I'd slit my wrists."

Aiden laughed. "There's a reason they dumped the job on me." Rolling his eyes, he added, "Give it to the kid who's fresh out of the Academy, because he'll do *anything*." He tapped the wheel with his thumbs. "I have to say, the threat assessments can be kind of fun, if only because they get my ass out of the office."

"What are those?"

"I go around the bases and check for security vulnerabilities. The paperwork afterward is a headache, but it's *not* a meeting and it's *not* sitting at my desk working on PowerPoint presentations." He turned to me briefly. "What about you?"

"Just a student right now. I'm about halfway through my bachelor's."

"Oh yeah? What's your major?"

I chuckled, hoping I didn't sound as self-conscious as I was. "Haven't declared one yet. I'm still trying to settle on something."

"Anything grabbing your interest?"

"Nothing that will ever keep my lights on, according to my father."

"Pfft." Aiden waved a hand. "Look, unless you're going into some specialized field like medicine or engineering, it really doesn't matter. Most of the corporate jobs out there? They couldn't care less if you majored in business administration or underwater basket-weaving as long as you have a degree."

"Really?"

Aiden nodded. "So what interests do you have that your dad doesn't think will keep the lights on?"

I shrugged. "Oh, you know. Mostly graphic design. Stuff like that."

"Graphic design?" He glanced at me, brow furrowed. "And he doesn't think that'll pay the bills?"

"He thinks it's one of those jobs where people just barely squeak by, living from freelance gig to freelance gig." Another shrug. "And a lot of them do. But I think I can pull it off." I pointed up ahead. "Take that left."

He turned, and I directed him down the short, meandering road to the parking lot. Aiden parked in the small lot that was surrounded on two sides by information placards, vending machines and snack shacks.

The wind was blowing just like it always was at Cape Hedo, but I loved it. The day was a hot one, and the wind kept it cool enough to be bearable. Perfect for an afternoon up here.

We followed a trail from the lot toward the cliffs, but before we'd gotten far, I stepped off the well-worn path. "This way."

"I...beg your pardon?"

I glanced back at him. "Come on. Trust me." He watched as I picked my way between plants and rocks toward the lip of the cliff.

"Shouldn't we stay on the path?" he called after me.

I turned around again. "You see any ropes or fences?"

"I... Well, no..."

"That's because there aren't any. Come on—the view is worth it."

He hesitated, then followed me.

"I like the lack of safety railings." I grinned at him as we neared the edge. "Lets me live dangerously."

Aiden laughed, approaching the cliff's edge but eyeing it nervously. "Doesn't seem like you let anything stop you from living dangerously."

"Okay, no, I don't. But seriously, wouldn't this place look stupid with railings all over it?"

He didn't stand quite on the edge and cautiously leaned forward, craning his neck to look over it.

I, of course, went all the way to the edge. The rocky lip was solid and stable enough, and as long as I kept my weight on my heels—and my center of gravity back *just* enough to balance me if a sudden wind tried to push me forward—I wasn't in any real danger.

This view never got old. Never. I could come up here every day between now and when I eventually left the island, and I'd still have to stop and stare out at the rocks and the water.

And what was I doing? Letting my gaze slide to the left and turning my head just enough to watch Aiden without him noticing. His T-shirt sleeve fluttered just enough to give me a glimpse of his toned arms—no ink or tan yet, but anyone who stayed here longer than a few months ended up with both eventually. His blond hair was short, but the wind still managed to play with it, which didn't help me with the whole quit-staring at-him thing.

Desperate for something else to talk about—and look at—I gestured at the horizon. "Sometimes, if it's really clear, you can see Yoron Island from here." I squinted, but there was a little bit of haze in the distance today. Just enough to hide the island.

"Anything interesting out there? At Yoron?"

"It's a good spot for spearfishing."

"Spearfishing?" Aiden's eyebrows jumped. "You've done that?"

"Couple of times. Last time, I got a little too close to a barracuda, and then a swarm of box jellies. I still snorkel and dive, but at least then I'm not focused on hunting, so I can actually see what else is around me." *Stop rambling, Connor.* "Anyway. Yeah. It's cool."

"Sounds like it. I'd like to give it a try someday. Minus the, uh, barracuda."

I laughed. "Yeah, I'd avoid those."

"Good idea." He scanned the horizon, taking in the scenery for the first time.

"What is that?" He gestured at the forested hills off to the right, and I knew before I looked what had caught his attention.

On top of one of the hills, partially hidden by the thick vegetation, was a huge bird statue. Black with the distinctive red beak and orange legs.

"That's a rail," I said. "One of those endangered flightless birds running around on the island."

"Interesting place for a statue. Doesn't seem like many people could see it unless they were up here."

"Actually, it's an observatory."

He turned his head. "Really?"

I nodded. "You can climb up in it and get a great view of Hedo. Want to check it out?"

"Hell, yeah."

The observatory wasn't far from Hedo. It had taken me a few tries to find it, but now I knew exactly which side road to take and where to turn to head up the steep, winding hill to the huge statue. Aiden parked, and we started up the stairs from the parking lot.

Up ahead, the giant bird came into view. Ass first, naturally, with the giant tail feathers throwing some shade over the stairs as we climbed higher.

As the stairs leveled out, Aiden looked up at the giant bird. "Wow. That's...insane."

"Right?"

"Can we go up in it?"

"Of course." I started toward the bird. "Let's go."

There was a staircase beside the bird in a building set up to look like a tree stump, and as we started up it, our footsteps echoed inside the hollow metal statue. Near the top, there was a window with a ledge big enough for two, maybe three people to sit comfortably.

I slid onto the ledge and sat with my legs dangling out the window.

A moment later, Aiden joined me. "Is this the top?"

"Not quite. We're right under its neck." I gestured up at the carved neck extending out above us, which led up to the bird's bright red beak.

Didn't matter that we weren't at the top, though. From here, we had an unobstructed view of Cape Hedo. The cliffs, the park, everything. The water was rough with huge swells and whitecaps. The tide peeled back to reveal the reefs, then rolled forward and slammed into the rock wall with a *pop* I could hear—and almost feel—from here.

"Doesn't look like great snorkeling conditions today," he said.

I shrugged. "Probably great conditions around the rest of the island, but you wouldn't want to snorkel Hedo anyway."

"Really? I thought you said you can't go wrong snorkeling off this island. Aside from spearfishing, anyway."

I shrugged. "Well, there's plenty to see out there, but look at the waves." As if on cue, a huge wave smacked against the cliffs even harder than before.

"Oh. Point taken."

We glanced at each other and both laughed quietly.

"You dive?" I asked.

Aiden shook his head. "Not yet. I'd like to learn, though. Eventually."

"Me too."

The conversation fell into a lull, but the silences between us weren't awkward. I wanted us to keep talking so I could get to know Aiden as much as possible, but it wasn't an uncomfortable silence that I needed to fill.

Eventually, Aiden gestured up at the neck of the statue above us. "You ever seen one of the rails? One of the real ones, I mean?"

"I've seen a few. If you know where to look, and you're patient, they're not too hard to find. Not too many left, though."

"There aren't?"

"No, they're really endangered because of the mongooses."

"Yeah?"

I nodded. "Some idiot decided the mongooses would be good for getting rid of the snakes."

"That worked in Hawaii, didn't it?"

"They were in Hawaii to eat rats, not snakes. But the idiots who brought them here didn't notice that Habu are nocturnal and mongooses aren't." I shook my head. "So then the mongooses figured out these flightless birds were an easier target."

"Guess they aren't stupid."

"Not when it comes to eating."

"Bet the birds wish they hadn't been quite so fucked by evolution."

I snorted. "No kidding."

We both laughed and then fell quiet. It wasn't an awkward silence. A thoughtful one, maybe—I had no idea what he had on his mind, but while my eyes were focused on the cliffs and ocean in front of us, my brain was completely tuned in to the man beside me.

After a while, Aiden turned to me. "Seems like you really know your way around this island."

"After this long, I'd better— Look!" I pointed out at the water and a jet of spray that had just shot up between the waves. "Did you see that?"

"See— Holy shit, is that a *whale?*"

"Actually, it's..." I watched for a second, and sure enough, another spray shot up. "Looks like it's a few whales."

"No way."

We both leaned forward, craning our necks as we held on to the edge of the window.

I scanned the water. "I hope they didn't go under. Could be an hour or more before they come back or—" Right then, a massive humpback came straight up out of the water, then flipped back, fins out to the sides just before it crashed back into the surf.

"Whoa!" Aiden's jaw dropped.

Another whale breached. Then a third. For a solid fifteen or twenty minutes, the whales played in the surf. I couldn't decide if there were three or four—there might've even been a fifth, but it was hard to keep track of all of them. One tail flipped up. Then another. As the water calmed, I sat back a little, stretching a crick out of my back.

"Looks like they're diving."

"Yeah?"

I nodded. "If they come back, it'll be a while."

"Damn. Still... That was the coolest thing I've ever seen."

"They're pretty cool, aren't they?"

"Very. You don't see stuff like that back home."

I looked out at the water. "So where is home?"

"The last few years, it was Annapolis." He shifted a little beside me, probably trying to get comfortable on the hard ledge. "Before that, I was born and raised in Las Vegas."

I turned to him. "Really? Wow."

He met my eyes. "Vegas isn't as great as it sounds. Trust me. Especially when you're a kid."

"So what *is* it like?"

"Hot. Dry. Crowded." He looked around. "I could really get used to this, believe me."

"You don't mind the humidity?"

"Nope. It's a hell of a lot worse in Maryland. There's no wind there, so the humidity just kind of...sits."

I wrinkled my nose. "Oh gross."

"Exactly." He turned to me. "What about you? Where are you from?"

"I'm a military brat. I'm 'from' everywhere." My gut tightened as soon as I said it. Things were going way too well tonight to ruin it with the usual what-branch-is-your-dad-in? line of questioning.

But just like yesterday, Aiden left the subject alone. We were quiet again, just watching the water and the scenery even though the whales were gone, and again, it wasn't awkward or uncomfortable. In fact, it was perfectly comfortable. I sometimes had this nervous need to fill silence even if there wasn't anything that needed to be said, but right then, I didn't. We were here, the view was gorgeous, and that was all that mattered.

I didn't realize how long we'd been up there until the sun was already inching down to the horizon.

I hadn't really started noticing sunsets until I came to Japan, but I couldn't imagine they were any more amazing anywhere else in the world. Watching the entire sky and the ocean change color, that always blew my mind. I could spend my entire life on this island and never get tired of watching the sun set into the ocean.

As the colors faded and the sky darkened, Aiden looked at his watch. "Damn. I guess we should head back eventually."

"Yeah." I glanced at him. "We can probably grab something to eat in Nago. There isn't much between here and there, and the snack shacks in the parking lot"—I gestured toward Hedo—"are probably closed."

"You know any places in Nago?"

I threw him a smug look. "Please. I know *all* the good places in Nago."

Aiden laughed. "Let's go, then." We climbed down from the window and started down the stairs. Over the echo of our footsteps inside the huge hollow structure, he said, "Thanks for bringing me up here, by the way."

"Thanks for coming with me."

He smiled, which made my blood pressure go haywire, especially when he quietly said, "Any time."

Chapter Five

Aiden

Connor was right: he knew where to find the good places in Nago. After an absolutely fantastic dinner at an amazing little ramen-noodle café, we headed back to my place.

By the time I steered us into the parking lot at the foot of my apartment, it was nearly eleven. We'd been together for hours, but it seemed like much less time had passed than that. I could've sworn he'd just arrived here, ready to take off to Cape Hedo, not that we had already been up there and back.

I turned the key, and the piece-of-shit engine shuddered once before falling silent. Disappointment tugged at my gut. This afternoon and evening had been amazing, and shutting off the engine seemed to underscore the fact that it was coming to an end. Maybe we could do it again, but I...I wasn't ready for tonight to be over.

Connor met my eyes. "So, um. If you want to check out anything else on the island, hit me up. I've been all over it."

"I'll do that. It's...nice to get out with someone who knows his way around." *It's also nice to have someone—* I cleared my throat and shifted my gaze away. As I unbuckled my seat belt, I said, "I guess I should let you get home."

Connor unbuckled his too. "Yeah. I guess so."

But neither of us moved.

We didn't say anything either. I caught myself wishing I'd left the engine idling. It wouldn't have made sense—I wasn't going anywhere after this—but would've at least filled the silence with something besides my own heartbeat.

Then Connor cleared his throat, the sound startling me. "I guess this is a little late in the game to ask, but..." He tapped his fingers rapidly beneath the passenger window.

I faced him. "Try me."

Chewing his lip, he met my eyes again in the near darkness. "Are you...uh...are you gay?"

My heart jumped into my throat. Any answer to a question like that could take this conversation down one of a few very, very different roads. I still had the proof of that above my eyebrow and on my knuckles.

Please tell me I haven't been misreading you.

I gulped. After a moment's hesitation, I nodded. "Yeah. I am."

Connor exhaled. "Good." And with that, he leaned across the console, and without any conscious thought on my part, my body moving as if there were something magnetic about him that drew me in whether I liked it or not, I met him halfway.

And he kissed me.

Oh my God.

Connor kissed me.

His lips were soft and tentative against mine. He didn't push for anything, didn't try to shove his tongue down my throat—in fact, he seemed perfectly content with a gentle, light kiss.

I reached up and touched the side of his neck, searching for more contact. As my fingertips drifted up his neck and into his hair, he exhaled through his nose, his breath cool and light on my cheek, and one of us—I had no idea who—deepened the kiss. Our lips parted, and goose bumps prickled my spine as my tongue slid past his.

His hand materialized on my waist, and as we pulled each other closer, it drifted toward the middle of my back. The console between us bit into my hip and couldn't have been comfortable for him either, but neither of us pulled away. The kiss went on, a kiss that didn't have to lead to anything else, without any pawing or groping or demanding. We touched, but it was gentle—the contact, like the kiss itself, happening for its own sake, without any obligation for more, even while every tremor and rapid heartbeat gave away how much I wanted him.

I was tempted to let my fingers drift downward, to see if he was as hard as I was, but I kept my hand on the back of his head. In my mind's eye, I saw us tumbling into bed together, naked and kissing, and still touching like this, still making out and letting everything else wait until we were good and ready for more. It was a fantasy—what guy would really be that patient?—but a hot one, and I couldn't help groaning softly into his kiss as the image played out in my head.

Connor's hand moved from my side to my chest, and then up to my neck, sliding around the back and mirroring the way I held on to him. Then, after God knew how much time had passed, he gently broke the kiss and touched his forehead to mine. "Holy fuck."

"Yeah. That." Wow, I was really out of breath. I drew back a little and opened my eyes, our surroundings slowly coming back into existence in my peripheral vision as I held his gaze in the low light. Head spinning and heart pounding, I swept my tongue across my tingling lips. "Do you, um, want to come inside?" I gestured at the stairwell in front of my car.

Connor glanced at the stairwell and gulped. For the first time all evening, he looked nervous. Really nervous. It was hard to tell in the low light, but I thought he might have paled a little.

"You don't have to." I touched his arm. "I'm not in any hurry."

He faced me again, and though his smile was nervous, it was genuine as far as I could tell. "I want to."

I didn't move. "Are you sure?"

Swallowing hard, he nodded.

"Don't be nervous," I whispered, cradling his face in both hands. "I don't bite. I promise."

He laughed softly. "What if I want you to?"

Oh. God.

I suppressed a shiver. "Well, that's different, isn't it?" And I kissed him again.

When I pulled away, he said, "I thought we were going upstairs?"

I laughed. "So we were."

So we did. Somehow, we made it from my car to my doorway, and I managed to get the key and the lock to work and let us inside.

As soon as the door was shut, Connor pulled me in for another kiss. It had only been a couple of minutes since that last kiss in the car, but now that he was kissing me again, it felt like it had been forever since we'd touched. Two minutes apart, and I fucking *missed* him, but he was against me again, holding on to me and kissing me like he'd been waiting all damned day for this.

I didn't even know what to do. Where I wanted to touch him, where to kiss him besides his amazing mouth. I didn't know if I wanted to fuck him or be fucked by him, only that I wanted us naked and moving together. I wanted to taste every inch of him, and I wanted to know what he felt like and sounded like when he reached that point when it was almost too much, that second before he let go, and I wanted to be holding on to him when he let go.

He pressed his hard cock against mine, and I gasped, breaking away from his kiss.

"Fuck..."

He said something I didn't understand, and his cock rubbed over mine through our clothes, and I somehow managed to say, "Bedroom might...might be more comfortable."

Connor shivered. "Where is it?"

I gestured down the short hall. "That—" And then he was kissing me again, guiding me blindly toward the hall, and I was so lost in his kiss I was almost lost in my apartment too, but between us, we made it into the bedroom.

We toed off our shoes—thank God we'd both worn sandals—as we fumbled and stumbled from the door to the bed.

Gravity shifted. The world tilted. Hell if I knew how or why, but we went from standing to lying on my bed, and I was in heaven. We weren't naked, but, my God, it was my fantasy come to life. Our bodies pressed together, our arms around each other, kissing like two men possessed, but still not groping and pawing at each other. We'd get there. We were both hard, both quivering all over, and still somehow managed to make out like we weren't in any hurry at all.

And then he rolled me onto my back and pinned me down. As he descended onto my neck, kissing so hard he was almost biting, I closed my eyes, my back arching under us.

"Oh God," I whispered. "You're a fucking top, aren't you?"

He froze.

So did I. "What? What's wrong?"

He lifted himself up. "Um..."

My heart pounded. Shit. What the hell? "Connor?" I touched his face. "What's wrong?"

"Nothing. Nothing. But I've, uh..." He exhaled and looked away. "I don't actually know. If I prefer top or bottom."

"So you're—" I paused. My heart sped up a little. "Is this...is this your first time?"

Color flooded his cheeks. "It's..."

I ran my fingers down his arm. "It's okay if it is. Just say so."

Connor swallowed hard. Then he nodded. "Yeah. It is. I'm—"

I cut him off with a kiss, wrapping my arms around him and pulling him against me. "I told you, it's okay."

He brushed my lips with his. "Probably should've told you before we...uh..."

"Don't worry about it." I ran my fingers through his hair. "I promise. It's okay."

He watched me uncertainly for a moment, then relaxed and leaned down to kiss me again. Then, with the most adorable, hopeful grin, he said, "You're not disappointed, are you?"

"Disappointed?" I pressed my hips against his. "Do I feel disappointed?"

Connor closed his eyes and bit his lip. "Fuck..."

"Out of curiosity, how much *have* you done?"

"Well." He laughed softly and met my eyes. "This."

"You've— Really?"

Connor nodded. As his cheeks darkened, he pulled away, avoiding my gaze now. "I know, it's kind of ridiculous for someone my age to—"

"No." I put a hand on his side, gently drawing him back to me. "There's no time limit on these things."

"But I don't have a clue what to...uh, what to do. I'm..." More redness flooded his cheeks.

"It's okay," I whispered. "All you have to do is tell me if you like something or if you want me to stop."

His eyes flicked back toward mine, an unspoken *really?* lifting his eyebrows.

I curved my hand around the back of his neck. His kiss was a little more tentative this time, but he relaxed against me and parted his lips for me.

Then I gently pushed him onto his back, and when I straddled him, he groaned as our cocks rubbed together through our clothes again. I kissed the side of his neck, working my way up to his ear. "I want you, but I don't want to go too fast." I pressed my lips to the edge of his jaw. "Just tell me if you want to stop."

He shivered but didn't speak.

I slid my hand over the front of his shorts, and we both gasped, the air rushing through the narrow sliver of space between his lips and mine. He pressed against my hand, and I squeezed gently as I kissed him.

"Clothes," he whispered. "We...should lose them."

Be still, my heart...

"You sure?"

He nodded and shot me the most devilish look. "They're kind of in the way, don't you think?"

"Yes. Yes, they are." I sat up and pulled off my shirt. As we stripped out of our clothes, I stole a glance at him, and...damn. I'd seen him without his shirt, but as he kicked off his shorts, my head spun. His narrow hips were sexy as hell, and his very erect cock was perfect. Not massive, but not lacking in the slightest—exactly the way I liked them.

On the bed, we came together again, and I rolled him onto his back. We made out and ground against each other, and I was so goddamned turned on there was only one thing I could think of.

"I want to make you come."

Connor moaned softly. "Jesus."

"Do you want me to?"

"Please."

Thank God. This wasn't too much for him. "Just...just tell me if I go too fast."

He nodded slightly and murmured, "I will."

I went extraslowly, moving down his chest and smooth abs one kiss at a time because I didn't want to overwhelm him, but he couldn't have known how much he overwhelmed me. Every time I touched him—with fingers, with lips—he responded as if I'd done so much more, shivering at a brush of my hand and arching his back at a soft kiss on his hip bone.

My lips were inches away from his cock when I looked up at him. "Am I going too fast?"

Eyes still closed, he shook his head. "No. Not...not too fast."

"Do you want more?"

"*Yes.*"

I watched his face as I ran the tip of my tongue along the underside of his cock. His eyes opened wide, his lips moving as if he couldn't decide between speaking or inhaling. I did it again, starting at the base and licking slowly, all the way up, and then slipping the head of his cock into my mouth.

"Oh. *Shit.*" A slow tremor went through him, his fingers closing around the sheets on either side of him as his hips lifted off the bed. "Jesus Christ."

I teased him with my lips and tongue, and then took him a little at a time, and as I did, his breathing quickened, turning to rapid, uneven gasps. His hand materialized on the back of my head—not pressing, just touching, bringing goose bumps to life all the way down the length of my spine. His fingers curled in my hair as if he was trying to grab on, though it wasn't quite long enough for that, and the way he kneaded my scalp made me shiver.

Propping myself up on one arm, I stroked him with my other hand. I'd intended to go slow, but the more I sucked his cock, the more turned on I was, and I couldn't help it. I gave him all I had, squeezing with my hand, fluttering my tongue, doing everything I knew to make him feel good, and every time he gasped or whimpered or swore softly, my own cock seemed to get even harder.

"I'm gonna...I'm gonna come." His fingers twitched in my hair. I stroked him faster and took him deeper into my mouth, and his helpless moan sent a shiver right through me. His whole body shook. His cock was even harder now, thicker, his hips moving like they wanted to thrust but didn't quite know how, and when I added the slightest twist to my strokes, he fucking lost his mind.

He thrust into my fist and my mouth, and semen jetted across my tongue so fast it almost caught me by surprise, but I recovered quickly and kept teasing him with my mouth and my hand until he whimpered for me to stop. I slowed my strokes and let him ease back down to earth before I let go completely.

Connor collapsed back on the mattress, shaking and panting. "Holy..."

I laughed. "You all right?"

"Uh-huh." He nodded and licked his lips. "Yeah. Yeah, I'm good. Jesus."

I settled beside him on my side. Tempting as it was, I hesitated to kiss him, not sure he'd be okay with kissing me after I'd sucked him off, but then he grabbed on to me and made short work of *that* illusion. He was panting, shaking, and his kiss was desperate and hungry, bordering on forceful, and I didn't think I'd ever been so goddamned turned on in my life. As worried as he was about being inexperienced, he was a living, breathing fantasy for me. This was all new to him. He wasn't mentally comparing me to other men. He was the most attractive man I'd ever met, and he was in my bed, and he was sweet and just the right balance of innocent and daring, and I wanted him so badly and in so many ways he couldn't possibly imagine.

Connor let his head fall back on the pillow and met my eyes. "That was so... I..." He swallowed. "I want to do the same for you, but I have no idea how."

"It's easier than it looks." I kissed him, letting it linger for a moment. "But it can wait until you want to. Until you feel comfortable, I mean."

"But you're..." His hand brushed my rock-hard cock, the light contact making me suck in a sharp breath. "I want to..."

And I need you to. So bad.

I lay on my side again. "Come here."

When he turned on his side, facing me, and slid closer, I guided his hand between us. As his fingers closed around my cock, he shuddered as if I'd been the one touching him. I encouraged him into motion, urging him to stroke me.

"Like that?" he asked.

"Yeah, like... Fuck. Like that." My hips were moving, pushing my dick through his fist in time with his tentative motions, and I wasn't going to last. No way in hell. I was just too turned on, with his hand on me and the taste of his orgasm on my tongue.

As he picked up speed, the friction edged toward uncomfortable, so I gently stopped him. "Wait," I murmured. I leaned away and picked up the bottle of lube I kept on the nightstand. "Use this." I popped the top, and he held out his hand. After I'd poured on a generous amount, he reached down again, and the cool liquid made me gasp. Connor stroked me slowly, but as the slick lube coated my cock, he did it faster, gripping a little tighter, and I almost lost my goddamned mind.

"Holy fuck," I moaned, thrusting into his fist.

"This good?"

I moaned again but couldn't form words. Desperate for something to hold on to, I grabbed the back of his neck, and when I dug my fingers in, he stroked even faster.

"Fuck. Oh fuck. That's..." I closed my eyes and let my head fall back. I kept fucking into his tight fist, my whole body trembling as I struggled just to remember to breathe.

"Oh my God," he whispered.

I forced my eyes open. One look at him—his own eyes wide, his lips apart like he was as blown away by this as I was—and I was gone.

"Fuck!" I tightened my grip on his neck and lost it. I probably cried out, but hell if I knew for sure. All I knew was how good this felt, how I couldn't remember the last time I'd come this hard, how fast the room was spinning as Connor kept stroking my cock. When it became too much, I clumsily grabbed his wrist. "S-stop."

He did, and my hand slid off his wrist, and when he loosened his grasp, I sank back onto the bed. "I can't believe you've never done that before."

He laughed shyly and followed me down. "Well, I'd never done it to anyone *else*..."

I met his eyes and made the connection. "Right. Got it."

"Practice makes perfect, eh?"

"Something like that." I curved my hand around the back of his neck and drew him all the way down. "Not that you need it, but you're welcome to practice on me *any* time." I lifted my head and kissed him lightly. "Because, at the risk of stating the obvious, I'd really like to see you again."

"Name the time and place."

"What would it take to talk you into my bed again?"

He shivered, a ragged breath whispering past my lips. "Okay, name the time."

"As soon as I get home from work tomorrow? Four thirty?"

"I'll be here."

Chapter Six
Connor

I couldn't sleep. I was more exhausted than I'd been since...since I didn't know when, but I was wide awake. An entire case of 5-hour Energy wouldn't have had my heart pumping like this at three in the morning.

Aiden, though?

Fuck.

Every time I closed my eyes, all I could think about was everything we'd done in my car and his apartment. A few times I thought I still felt my lips tingling from kissing him.

And, my God, we hadn't stopped at kissing. If we'd had all night and I'd had a little more nerve, we might've gone even further. Hell, my head was still spinning just from the things we *had* done.

The blowjob was fucking amazing, but I hadn't expected to be so turned on while I was jerking him off. That was incredible. Watching him fall apart like that, knowing I was even capable of having that effect on a man, had been unreal. I'd been scared out of my mind—What if I was clumsy? What if I did it wrong? What if he got bored?—but the next thing I knew, Aiden was arching against me, holding on to me and shaking and coming.

I'd kissed a few guys before, though I hadn't gone much further than that, and Aiden was just...amazing. One kiss, and I'd have done just about anything he asked me to do. In the light of day, that spooked me, but at the same time made me want him more. I'd been wrapped around his finger and would have done anything and everything he wanted me to, but he hadn't pushed. Not even a little. I'd thought a lot about what it might feel like to be with someone physically, but never thought I'd describe it as safe. But that was how I felt with Aiden. I felt safe.

I felt safe when I was with him, and completely distracted when I wasn't. All I could think about was Aiden. I hadn't been this wrapped up in a guy since high school, when one of those all-consuming crushes could keep me up for hours every night. And that was before we'd... God, last night had really happened, hadn't it? We'd been naked, and kissing, and then he'd...

I shivered at the thought. Yeah, it had really happened. I hadn't been able to stop thinking about it since I'd left his place, and now, every time I closed my eyes, I saw Aiden's head bobbing up and down over my dick, and I felt the electricity shooting up my spine each time his tongue slid across my skin.

Fuck. I was just a few hours from seeing Aiden, and a hell of a lot of studying away from being done for the day. And with a hard-on like this? I wasn't getting a damned thing done.

I pushed my chair back from my desk, stood—carefully— and moved to my bed. Now that I wasn't fighting it anymore, there was no turning back. As I unzipped my shorts, my dick was so hard it was almost painful, and my head was spinning. Somehow, I was already out of breath, which made me think of Aiden panting against me, which didn't help at all.

I pushed my shorts and boxers down just enough to get them out of the way. Then I poured some lotion on my hand and wrapped my fingers around my cock. Eyes closed, I let my thoughts go right back to last night, and as I stroked myself, I tried to remember exactly how he'd moved his hand, but all I could think of was what he'd done with his mouth. I'd always figured a blowjob would be hot—obviously—but I'd never imagined the mind-blowing things he'd do with his lips and tongue.

And then he'd been next to me, his dick in my hand and his whole body reacting to my touch. In my mind, I saw him closing his eyes and gasping. I felt more than heard him groan, and I remembered the wet heat of his semen in my hand and on my stomach as he came, and my back arched off my bed as his orgasm replayed in my head over and over again.

It really happened. It was real.

And tonight we'll...

I couldn't even finish the thought before my eyes rolled back. I came so hard my toes curled and my hips lifted up off the bed, and the semen in my hand and on my stomach reminded me all over again of Aiden's, and I fell apart a little more.

And then I was still. Shaking and panting, but, otherwise, I couldn't move. Not while the aftershocks ricocheted through me.

When I'd finally calmed down and wasn't quite so hypersensitive, I carefully released my cock and grabbed some tissues off the nightstand. My hands were shaking almost as badly as they had when I'd been with Aiden earlier, but I managed to wipe them off and get the tissues into the trash can.

Then I collapsed back on the bed.

Now that I didn't have that distracting hard-on to occupy my thoughts, I could think a bit more clearly. For the moment, anyway. Wasn't like this was the first time I'd had to jerk off today, but it had better be the last. After all, I was seeing Aiden again tonight.

I shivered. As hot as last night was, I regretted we hadn't gone any further. Maybe it would have been too far, too fast, but every time I played out in my head what we could have done, I kicked myself for being so scared and inexperienced.

Still, Aiden had been awesome. He didn't act for a second like he was impatient with me, or like he was bored. And, God, that blowjob...

I shivered and leaned back against my headboard. I so wanted to do that for him. He hadn't seemed the least bit unsatisfied with the hand job I'd given him, but there was no way in hell it had been as good as the blowjob he'd given me. And if we had sex...

"You're a fucking top, aren't you?"

Was I? I'd fantasized about being on the top and being on the bottom, but when it came down to the real thing, I had no idea what I wanted. The thought of fucking someone turned me on so much I couldn't think, but what about taking him? The porn I'd sneaked onto my laptop sure made it look like the guy on the bottom was having a good time. Then again, I doubted any of them were virgins. Not even the guys in the it's-his-first-time-getting-fucked videos. They were real virgins like the guys in army porn were real soldiers.

And whether I was a top or a bottom, the fact was I had no idea what I was doing. Oh, I had the kissing thing down. And a hand job was pretty much a given. Anal sex or a blowjob? Not a clue.

My gaze drifted toward my laptop. Then I glanced at the door but felt like an idiot. I was an adult. Living in my father's home, yes, but a grown-ass adult. If I wanted to look at porn—or something a bit more "educational"—that was my own damned business.

I got up off the bed and moved back to my desk. I minimized the paper I was supposed to be working on and opened my browser. For a good minute, I watched the cursor blinking in the search engine before I finally started typing. My face burned as the words appeared on the screen: *How to give a blowjob.*

I was probably going to regret it, but I hit Search and watched the results pile up.

Some of the articles were hilariously technical.

Firmly grasp the shaft with one hand. Move hand in an up-and-down motion, and at the same time, insert the head between your lips.

Really, guys?

The accompanying instructional video was even better, with a guy pantomiming a blowjob over another guy who was fully dressed. Because God forbid an actual penis appear in a video about how to suck cock.

Another site was definitely more graphic but not all that useful. It had a bunch of pictures that looked less like someone giving a blowjob and more like some dude—or chick—unhinging his jaw and choking on one of those gigantic Hickory Farms salamis. Hot.

Another harped on the idea that the only way to give a decent blowjob was to shove a finger up the recipient's ass. In fact, it was more of a fingering tutorial than a blowjob tutorial, so why the hell didn't it just call itself that?

Shaking my head, I clicked to another site.

If your partner is exceedingly large, you may find him difficult to accommodate comfortably...

Followed by another Hickory Farms gag-a-thon.

I rolled my eyes and closed that window too. Apparently porn was my best bet after all. At least then I could see what the guys were doing *and* not be subjected to something that sounded like a Craftsman manual. There had to be something that—

A knock at my door made me jump. My hackles went up, and I quickly minimized the website as I muttered, "It's open."

My father pushed open the door. He didn't come inside. I wasn't really sure why not. He'd already interrupted me. Why not intrude a little more?

"What's up?" I asked.

God. That look. The everything-you-say-can-and-will-be-used-against-you look. "What time did you get home last night?"

I ground my teeth. The fifteen-year-old in me who was still afraid of breaking his curfew wanted the ground to open up and swallow me before my dad figured out I was seeing someone. The adult who was damned tired of being treated like a kid wanted to snap back with something snide like *I was out getting my dick sucked.*

As calmly as I could, I closed my textbook, using my notes as a bookmark. Then I faced my dad. "Do I have a curfew?"

"Of course not." He slid his hands into his pockets and narrowed his eyes slightly. "I'm just curious where you were."

"Out."

"With?"

"Dad, do—"

"Who were you with, Connor?"

"Who says I was with anyone?" My heart pounded. Dad had lectured me a hundred times about focusing on my studies and not getting caught up in dating. Specifically, not dating anyone in the military. Which meant dating precisely no one on Okinawa.

"If you don't like the rules, you don't have to stay here."

I clenched my jaw. We both knew damn well I didn't have a choice. This wasn't my only option, but it was by far my best one.

"I was just out by myself, all right?" I said quietly. "I needed a break from studying, so I went up to Cape Hedo."

His eyebrow rose. "Until midnight?" Before I could answer, though, he waved a hand. "Just let me know if you're going to be out so late, all right? I like to know if someone's going to be coming in at all hours of the night."

I'm sure *that's why you care if I'm out late.*

"Yeah. Okay."

He nodded once and then left, and as soon as he'd disappeared down the hall, I groaned and rubbed a hand over my face. I hated being in this position. Fucking hated it.

What choice did I have, though? In order to avoid crippling student debt, I was going to school via Dad's GI Bill, and the condition of using that had been that I lived at home until I graduated. To save money, he'd insisted. Some days, I wondered if it was just a ploy to keep me here until he absolutely had to let me grow up and move out.

I could move out now. Fly back to the States, find a place of my own, get my shit together. And then what? With the economy the way it was, someone with a high school diploma and precisely zero marketable skills would be lucky to get a minimum-wage job, and flipping burgers wouldn't get me through college, never mind pay rent. Finishing college? Not a chance.

So I was stuck here. And I was grateful, of course. Our arrangement let me focus solely on my classes and still have some downtime in between, rather than working three jobs just to make ends meet and falling asleep during exams.

Most importantly, it meant I didn't have to fall back on the other option: living with my mother. Dad knew as well as I did that I wouldn't go there voluntarily, and for all his you-don't-have-to-live-here crap, I knew damn well he'd never force me to go. For that matter, he'd probably do everything in his power to keep from *letting* me live with her.

But whether or not living with my mother was an option, everything came down to one simple thing: I could either live with my father here on Okinawa, or I could go back to the States and be out on my ass.

Like it or not, I didn't have a choice.

Chapter Seven
Aiden

My heart was going ninety miles an hour. Connor was on his way over, and I was on my way out of my mind from anticipation and nerves and horniness and—

Jesus. Get a grip.

My phone vibrated.

On my way up.

I jumped off the couch and headed for the door, and as I pulled it open, Connor came around the top of the stairwell. I reached for him, slid a hand around the back of his neck and pulled him into a kiss.

My whole body immediately responded. I'd already been nearly hard just knowing he was on his way up the stairs, and pressed against him now, my cock hardened completely. My heart was racing, my legs shaking, and it was all I could do not to drop to my knees and suck him off right then and there. If I hadn't had a nice old lady living next door, I probably would have done exactly that.

Connor raked his fingers through my hair, and then broke the kiss. "I couldn't study at all today," he panted against my lips. "Couldn't fucking concentrate."

"I've been...all day. Thinking." The words barely came out at all. Getting them in order was asking too much. "About this."

"Me too." Connor tugged my shirt free from my shorts. "We should go inside."

"We should." I grabbed his belt and pulled him toward me.

We stumbled across the threshold. He kicked the door shut behind us, and now that we were inside, away from any prying eyes, we didn't hold back. I shoved him up against the wall beside the door. He pressed his rock-hard cock against mine, moaning softly into my kiss.

"I don't want to go too far tonight," I said. "I don't...I don't want to push you."

He shook his head, sliding his hands down my sides to my hips. "You're not. I want this." He leaned in and kissed me again. "I want you."

I shivered. "It's mutual."

"Good."

"Seemed like you enjoyed last night."

Connor shivered. "I loved it."

"I want to do it again."

He moaned. "Please."

"Just tell me—" I ran out of air. "Just tell me if we're going too fast."

Connor nodded. "I will."

His hand slid between us and over the front of my shorts, and we both groaned softly as he squeezed my erection.

Stroking me through my clothes, he murmured, "I have no idea what I'm doing."

"You're doing fine." I was already out of breath? Jesus. "Trust me. You're doing *just* fine."

Connor gave a soft little moan and kissed me again. As he stroked me and kissed me, I tried to get out of my clothes. I wanted to be close to him, touching skin to skin, and, damn it, I should've worn a T-shirt. This one had too damned many buttons. And why the fuck had I worn a belt? Why had he worn one?

Whatever.

A buckle jingled. His shirt found its way to the floor by our feet. Another buckle. Somehow I managed to get his zipper down, and somehow he managed to get a few buttons open on my shirt.

And we were still against the wall by the door.

"We should..." I leaned down and kissed his neck and, for a moment, completely forgot what I'd been trying to say. "The bedroom. We should"—God, his skin was hot—"go in the bedroom."

Connor exhaled. "You keep doing that," he murmured, "and we're not going to make it past your couch."

I pressed against him and kissed his neck again. "You say that like it's a bad thing."

"Not at—"

Bang! Bang! Bang!

Connor jumped. "What the hell?"

I glared at the door. "Seriously?"

Bang! Bang! Bang!

"Maybe you should get that." Connor slid a hand over the front of my pants. "And if we have to, we'll just start over."

God, the way he touched me...

But he was right. We could just start over. And whoever was at the door was damned persistent.

"Good idea." I kissed him lightly. "Don't move."

"I won't. Much."

I kissed him once more, and then pushed myself off him.

Bang! Bang! Bang!

"I'm coming, I'm coming," I grumbled. "This had better be fucking important."

I turned the dead bolt and, with one hell of a tirade waiting on the tip of my tongue, pulled open the door.

And my stomach dropped into my feet. "General Bradshaw?"

From behind me, "*Dad?*"

I whipped around, eyes wide and jaw open. "What?"

Connor's face reddened. He looked at me, then past me, then at me again.

Slowly, I faced General Bradshaw. Every unfastened button felt so conspicuous they might as well have been on fire. The hard-on wasn't such an issue anymore, but the unbuckled belt and the half-untucked shirt were damning enough. Connor's shirt at our feet and his partially unzipped shorts left absolutely no room for doubt. There was no pretending we'd just been talking or that he'd been here for any purpose other than ripping each other's clothes off and doing what came naturally.

"Let's go, Connor," Bradshaw said coldly.

"Let's— How did you find me?" Connor shook his head. "And why the hell did you? I'm a grown-ass adult!"

"I followed you." He said it so calmly, so matter-of-factly, as if following his son to my apartment was a perfectly logical, rational thing to do. My blood turned cold. If he'd followed Connor, then he'd been here the whole time. Which meant he'd seen us at my door. He'd seen us kissing and then stumbling in through the door. As if our disheveled clothes weren't incriminating enough.

Bradshaw gestured sharply at his son. "Let's go."

Connor planted his feet, staring incredulously at his father. "Are you really going to forbid me to see him? I'm not fifteen, you know."

"No, you're not." Bradshaw turned to me, his hard eyes making my blood run cold. "Stay away from my son, Ensign."

"Are you kidding me?" Connor snapped. "Dad, I'm—"

"Leaving." Bradshaw glared at his son. "That's what you're doing."

"Are—"

"Get out of here, Connor."

"Dad, I'm—"

"And you, Ensign." Bradshaw faced me and stabbed his finger at my chest. "I mean it. You'll stay the hell away from my son. That's an order."

I looked at Connor. Then Bradshaw. Then Connor again. Good God, how had I not noticed? The general's hair was buzzed short, but where it hadn't grayed, it was the same dark brown as his son's. They both had the same blue eyes. Connor was leaner, Bradshaw more grizzled, but they were unavoidably father and son.

Connor held my gaze, his eyes pleading, but for what? For me to ignore his father? For me to slam the door in the man's face? For forgiveness?

"Connor." His father beckoned sharply. "I'll see you at home."

Connor's eyes flicked back and forth from his father to me. Then he sighed, scooped his shirt up off the floor and brushed past me with a whispered "I'm sorry."

I wanted to reach for him and stop him, but I couldn't move. I was just caught off guard. Way off guard.

Connor, wait...

General...

The door closed.

I sagged against the wall and exhaled.

Connor must have been mortified. I would have been.

In fact, I was. And I was terrified. I rubbed both hands over my face, wincing as my fingers aggravated the stitches and bruises.

Fuck. So much for no one in my chain of command knowing I was gay. With DADT in the past, I didn't *have* to hide my sexuality at work, but I chose to because it was none of anyone's business. That, and with or without DADT, there was still some hostility toward gays. I knew for a fact that Commander Morris was an outspoken homophobe, and the less he knew about me, the better.

But if my sexuality came out, it wasn't the end of the world. A headache, yes, but something I could live with. Dating the son of a man who had the power to make my career hell? That was an entirely different thing. He couldn't officially punish me for it, but he had clout. He had connections.

Christ.

Less than two months on this fucking island, and I'd found two men who'd piqued my interest.

One had put me in the emergency room.

The other was General-fucking-Bradshaw's son.

Chapter Eight
Connor

I was too numb to do anything but let my dad's taillights lead me back to Kadena.

Damn it. Fucking damn it. I'd finally connected with a guy, and now this. What the hell? On one hand, I couldn't believe my father had followed me to Aiden's place and dragged me out like that. On the other...

Hell. I wasn't surprised.

At every single stoplight, I debated flipping a bitch and going straight back to Aiden's. What was the point, though? Dad knew where he lived. Judging by how terrified Aiden had looked when Dad had ordered him away from me, he'd probably shoo me out of his apartment anyway.

I couldn't blame him. From what I'd seen and heard, Dad was *that* officer at the command. He said "jump", they all said "how high?". And when he said "stay the fuck away from my son", a smart ensign said "yes, sir". The fact that I was an adult who could just as easily tell him to fuck himself was a moot point.

Sighing, I thumped my hand against the steering wheel.

Go fuck himself? Yeah. Like it was that simple. I was a dependent, and damn if I didn't fit that title to the letter. He knew it. I knew it. And that was why I was still behind him as we pulled into the main gate of Kadena Air Base.

He slowed a little while the sentry checked my ID, and waited for me to catch up with him. Bastard. Wasn't like I didn't know how to get home. He had to know as well as I did that I wasn't going to defiantly turn around, screech my tires and take off. That ship had sailed about ten stoplights ago.

We turned off the main road and into Officer Housing, winding up the familiar road to the house. Dad pulled his car into the garage, and I parked mine in its usual spot beside the house. I hoped I could slip in through the front door and disappear into my bedroom—Jesus, was I still sixteen or something?—and avoid my father, but he headed me off in the living room.

"We need to talk."

"No, we don't." I tried to step around him, but he sidestepped and blocked me. He didn't touch me, didn't even reach for me, but damn if he didn't stop me in my tracks. "Dad, I don't want to talk about this."

"Tough shit," he growled. "What the hell were you doing over there?"

"Do you really want the details?" I snapped. "It's none of your fucking business who I date or what I do with—"

"It is as long as you are a dependent living under my roof," Dad threw back. "And as long as you are, you're not dating anyone who's under my command."

"Which rules out about ninety percent of the men on this fucking island, doesn't it? Unless you want me trolling Futenma for Marines?"

Dad glared at me. "I want you focusing on your studies."

"Every minute of every day? Jesus fucking Christ, I'm—"

"Watch it, Connor."

I gritted my teeth. Trust the son of a bitch to make me feel two inches tall. Or twelve years old. Calmer now—well, quieter, at least—I said, "So what do I do? Just throw myself at the books for the next two years and not date anyone at all?"

Dad exhaled. "Look, I'm sorry. I don't believe for a second this is easy."

"Then why do you—"

"We've been over this," he snapped, tensing up again. "And we're not discussing it now." He stabbed a finger at me. "Just stay away from Ensign Lange."

At the mention of Aiden's name, the floor dropped out of my anger and my heart dropped into my feet. I should've known things wouldn't work with him. Didn't think Dad would be the one to interfere, but sooner or later, something would've fucked it up.

I just shook my head. "I don't think I need to. You put the fear of God into him, so I doubt he'll come anywhere near me." I looked my dad in the eye. "Mission accomplished, eh?"

With that, I stepped around him and stormed out of the room. Upstairs, I salvaged what little pride I had left and closed the bedroom door as gently and quietly as I could, refusing to give him a second to believe I was still the petulant teenager he seemed to think I was. Yeah, I was pissed. Yeah, I was frustrated. But I wasn't resorting to slamming doors.

Alone behind a closed door, I took a long, deep breath and slowly let it out. This arrangement with my dad had already been about to drive me insane, but now? Fuck.

And it wasn't like I could move out. Either I lived here with my dad, or I went back to the States. Going back to the States meant living with my mother, which was absolutely not an option, and I couldn't afford to live on my own yet. Here on Okinawa, employment opportunities for dependents were slim, and most of my time was devoted to college anyway, so I hadn't been able to come up with much in the way of savings.

I wasn't sixteen anymore, but damn if I wasn't still completely dependent on my dad. Under his roof and under his thumb. I had a car, a license and no curfew, but I may as well have been as tethered to this house as my two-year-old half sister.

I stood at my window and stared out at the view of the East China Sea. Now that the confrontation was over, my mind wandered back to everything Aiden and I had been doing before my dad interrupted. I wondered what we'd be doing right then if we'd been left to our own devices. We would've been naked by now, no doubt. Then again, Aiden seemed to enjoy taking his time. For all I knew, we'd probably just be getting to his bedroom. And he'd be whispering in my ear what he was going to do to me. Or maybe his mouth would already be on my cock.

I shivered at the thought. God, I wanted him.

This couldn't be over yet. No way. Dad had vetoed a thing or two in my life, and more than one guy had shied away as soon as he knew my father was That Guy, but I couldn't accept that I'd lost someone like Aiden that easily.

It was probably a long shot, but I'd never been able to resist long shots anyway, so I pulled out my phone and texted him: *Sorry about my dad. Had no idea he'd fucking follow me like that.*

I didn't expect a response. He'd probably deleted me from his phone by now and would delete that message faster than he'd stomp on a cockroach. Less than a minute later, though, my phone buzzed, and a text came through: *It's ok.*

A second or two after that: *This could make things complicated.*

I sighed with tentative relief. Maybe he was still on board with seeing each other after all, even if it meant a little extra discretion.

Gnawing my lip, I wrote: *I'd still like to see you.*

A long, long moment went by after I sent the message, and my heart pounded harder and harder with every second that passed.

When my phone buzzed again, it startled me so badly I almost dropped it.

I'm off work at 4 tomorrow. Meet somewhere away from the base?

My heart fluttered, but my stomach was still in knots. *I don't want to get you in trouble.*

The next message came through, and it took a full minute before I could even look at it. I was sure I already knew what it would say. It had to be *Yeah, you're probably right* and *It was fun while it lasted.*

I looked at the screen: *Don't worry about it. We'll be discreet.*

Closing my eyes, I held my cell phone in both hands and whispered, "Thank God."

Then I sent back: *Meet at your place around 1630?*

Thirty seconds later, he replied: *I'll see you then.*

With things more or less settled between me and Aiden, I put the phone aside, reopened my textbook and tried to study. After all, it wasn't like I had any plans for the evening now, and I did have an exam coming up, not to mention a research paper due soon. Might as well use the rest of my evening to make some headway on the work I would not be doing tomorrow night.

Should've known it was pointless, though. The words on the page kept reorganizing themselves so all I could read was one simple phrase: *I'll see you then.*

Shoving my books aside, I leaned back and stared out the window. I was ahead in this class anyway, and the exam wasn't until next week. I had time. Of course, I was fooling myself if I thought I'd be able to concentrate any better after I saw Aiden tomorrow, but right now the pins and needles and butterflies were just too much.

I had until tomorrow afternoon to cook up an excuse. *My study group is meeting. I'll be at the library.* Something I could leave on a note before Dad got home. I'd thought about having Hitomi pass the message on to him, but she didn't need to be caught in the middle of this.

I'd figure it out. Somehow, I'd come up with something, buy myself a few hours and meet up with Aiden. Maybe we'd talk about tonight. Maybe we'd both finally come to our senses and realize there was no doing this behind Dad's back.

Maybe we'd make up for the time we'd lost tonight.

Whatever. I'd see him. Nothing else mattered.

I'll see you then.

Chapter Nine
Aiden

Department-head meetings were hell. Always. Nothing was more boring than listening to blowhards ramble on about what was going on in their respective departments.

Even better, being the lowest man on the totem pole by at least three or four pay grades, I always had to get there early to make sure the coffee was ready. Woe be unto me if a CO came in at 0645 to an empty coffeepot.

But this morning's meeting had to be the worst one ever. Even worse than the time Admiral Horton had droned on for a full hour in that god-awful monotone of his about something nobody cared about. I'd wanted to stab myself in the jugular with a pen about ten minutes into that, and after an hour, I was pretty sure I wasn't alone.

Today, though, I'd have given my right arm to listen to Horton ramble. Why? Because I was sitting right across from General Bradshaw. He'd come in a few minutes before the meeting started and, glaring at me the entire time, had taken the chair opposite mine. There was no tactful way to casually get up and take a seat that took me out of his line of sight.

I stared into my coffee cup. Then at the table. I focused hard on my pen, analyzing every piece of microscopic text as if I were observing an alien spacecraft. Anything to keep from looking at the man directly across from me.

He wasn't going to let this go. No way. God only knew the conversation he'd had with Connor last night, and I was dreading the one he'd have with me. It was weird to be worried about this shit in my twenties instead of my teens, but...there I was.

Two chairs down, Commander Yates stopped talking. I hadn't heard a word he said—didn't even realize he was giving his briefing until he'd stopped—but as he fell silent and closed the file folder in front of him, my mind checked back into the meeting.

Beside me, Colonel Patterson tapped a pen on a yellow legal pad. "Thank you, Commander. And what about the Antiterrorism Department?" He turned to me. "Ensign Lange?"

I gulped. I'd long ago gotten over my nerves when it came to speaking in front of officers who outranked me, like this group did, but I couldn't say the same about speaking in front of the man who'd caught me with his half-dressed son and a hard-on.

I gave my brief, and, unlike some of the other guys here, I kept mine *brief*. It was dull enough—a list of threat assessments completed in the past week, a rundown of scheduled assessments for the next one, a few comments on some concerns raised about local nationals photographing our aircraft from just outside the fence—without droning on for twenty minutes. That, and the higher-ups preferred to hear themselves talk, not the "shiny new ensign", as they liked to call me.

And even if I'd been one of the long-winded guys, I was keeping this as short as possible today because, Jesus fuck, this meeting needed to be over before Bradshaw lost his shit and choked me. Which he'd probably do sooner or later anyway. Fuck.

I finished my briefing. A few of the other department heads gave theirs. During his, Bradshaw gave no indication that anything was out of the ordinary. Well, aside from the ball-withering look he gave me after he finished.

And then the meeting was over. Time to face the general.

Except someone else grabbed him. As much as I was dreading the inevitable confrontation, I wasn't the least bit relieved when Captain Warren and Colonel Patterson asked Bradshaw to join them for another brief—yeah, right—meeting. They'd be awhile. They always were. And that meant another hour or two for me to get wound up and anxious and freak myself the fuck out over crossing paths with the general.

I went back to my office, ostensibly to get some work done. That was about as likely as Bradshaw's meeting being short and sweet. Sitting in my chair, staring at the computer screen and stacks of paperwork, I barely even remembered what I did for a living. All I could think about was what happened last night and the fallout that was most definitely on its way.

The day after I met Connor, I hadn't struggled to concentrate like I did today. I was fucked. So fucked. Officially, there was nothing Bradshaw could do—his son was of age, DADT was history and everything had been consensual—but he had clout and connections. Someone with his time and service, especially now that he was that far up the food chain, had friends in high places. And probably some low ones. God knew how many favors he had yet to cash in.

Scrubbing a hand over my face, I whispered a string of profanity. Aside from my inevitable demise when Bradshaw got out of his meeting, there was one other thing I couldn't stop thinking about.

Connor.

God, Connor.

Even while the adrenaline had been pumping last night, when I'd been sure Bradshaw was about to rip me to pieces right then and there, I'd been disappointed as hell that Connor and I had been interrupted. I had no idea how far we would have gone if left to our own devices, but I desperately wanted to pick up where we'd abruptly left off. Consequences be damned, I wanted him. Badly.

But how did he feel about things now? And seriously, *was* his father going to turn me into shark chum?

I pulled my phone out of my desk drawer and sent Connor a text: *Why do I get the feeling your dad is going to kill me today?*

I really, really hoped for a response of: *LOL. His bark is worse than his bite.*

Instead, he said: *Sorry. :-(I should have told you.*

Sighing, I rubbed my eyes. Yeah, it would've been nice if he'd told me, but I couldn't blame him. I'd have been lying if I said our encounter at Hiji Falls would've lasted past the parking lot if I'd known that cute kid in the pool was General Bradshaw's son.

Then I texted back: *It's not your fault.*

It wasn't his fault. Of course it wasn't. And if he'd warned me, then we never would've kissed like that, and I never would've been in bed with him, naked and sweating when he came.

I shivered.

Right then, my phone vibrated again.

If this is a deal breaker, it's ok.

No, it's not, I quickly responded. *I still want to see you.*

It *should* have been a deal breaker. If I had any sense at all, it would have been. But everything about Connor added up to something I didn't want to miss out on. And that kiss...

Shivering again, I sent him another message: *Are we still on for tonight?*

He didn't respond right away. Maybe he was in class. Or driving. Or just scared shitless.

Whatever the case, I couldn't just sit there staring at my phone. I needed to get some work done. Pushing my phone aside, I tried to focus on that and not obsess over Connor's answer or lack thereof.

The stack of folders on my desk may as well have been a Habu, coiled up and ready to bite my hand. Sooner or later, I'd have to finish all of it, but that meant delivering everything to various people. Colonel Patterson. Captain Warren.

And General Bradshaw.

Fuck. I could only hide in my office for so long. Sooner or later—

The ringing phone just about sent me tumbling out of my chair. I muttered a few curses, took a second to collect myself, and picked it up.

"ATO office, Ensign—"

"My office."

I closed my eyes and mouthed *fuck* before I said, "Be right there, sir."

The line went dead. Crap. So much for putting this off.

I left the office before I could talk myself out of it and followed the hallway to the door with the familiar brass nameplate—*General D. M. Bradshaw.*

The guys around the department had told me that everyone here eventually got chewed out in this office for something or another. Pretty sure none of them had "he caught you getting ready to put your dick in his son" on the list of possible charges.

I took a deep breath, set my shoulders back and tapped on the door.

"Come in."

I glanced skyward, asked anyone who was listening for anything I could get—strength, wisdom, invisibility—and pushed the door open.

General Bradshaw looked up at me, and his eyes narrowed. "Have a seat, Ensign."

I'd rather not...

"Sir, I—"

"This will only take a moment." His words had just enough of an edge to let me know that "have a seat" hadn't been an invitation or a request.

"Yes, sir," I murmured and obeyed the order.

He stared at me for a long moment. Just like in the meeting this morning, his expression was icy. No two ways about it—his eyes scared the shit out of me.

Bradshaw's voice was cool and even when he spoke. "You're an Academy grad, aren't you, Ensign?"

I nodded. "Yes, sir."

"So you've probably got a grand plan for your career." He got up and came around the desk. "You've probably got your eye on commanding a boat or two, don't you? Making admiral, maybe?"

Of course I'd dreamed about eventually manning the helm of an aircraft carrier and ultimately retiring with a couple of stars on my shoulder. Suddenly I felt those dreams dangling over my head like a cat's plaything, ready to be jerked out of my grasp if I reached for them. Or reached for Connor, as it were.

"Yes, sir," I whispered, my mouth dry.

He nodded slowly and leaned against his desk, hands folded beneath his shiny belt buckle. "I'm sure I don't have to tell you that a couple of phone calls could end your shiny post-Academy career before it gets started."

I swallowed.

"Or," he went on, "I'm sure it would only take a few more calls to find out if there's room for an antiterrorism officer in, say, Bahrain."

My stomach flipped.

"Maybe even Diego Garcia." A faint smirk formed on his lips, which turned my spine to ice. "Do you know what there is on Diego Garcia, Ensign?"

Completely mute, I shook my head.

"Nothing. Not a single goddamned thing." He inched closer, looming over me. "But with the right motivation, I'm sure the base there could find something for you to do. Am I understood?"

Still unable to speak, I nodded.

Bradshaw regarded me silently. My heart beat so hard I was sure he could hear it, and my stomach must've done twelve somersaults while he just stood there staring down at me. Finally, he said, "Listen, what you do in your personal life, and who you do it with, that's none of my business. I couldn't care less. *But*"—he stabbed a finger at me—"that ends the second my son gets involved."

I unstuck my tongue from the roof of my mouth and croaked, "Understood, sir."

"Good. Now get the fuck out of my office, and don't let me even *think* you've been anywhere near Connor, or so help me, you'll be on a plane to Diego Garcia so fast your head will spin."

He pointed at the door, and with a muttered "Yes, sir" I got the fuck out of his office.

As soon as I was safely down the hall, I stopped. I leaned against the wall and closed my eyes. Jesus Christ. I'd thought my years of worrying about parental approval and sneaking around with guys were long since over. Evidently, I was wrong.

And maybe it was my mile-wide stubborn streak, or maybe it was the fact that I'd been intrigued by Connor from day one, but even after facing off with the general in his office, even while my pulse was still pounding and my stomach was still turning, obeying Bradshaw was out of the question.

Send me to Diego Garcia if you want, asshole. I need to finish what Connor and I started.

The thought sent yet another shiver through me.

"You all right, Ensign?"

I looked up to see Commanders Connelly and Mays coming down the hall with coffee cups in their hands. "Yeah, just, uh..." I nodded toward Bradshaw's office and grimaced. "Just finished getting my ass chewed."

Mays laughed and clapped my shoulder. "And you're still alive. Congrats, Ensign. You're a man now."

Shane chuckled, but something in his expression unnerved me. Especially when he glanced at Mays. "Go on ahead. I'll catch up with you."

Mays nodded and kept walking.

As soon as the other commander was gone, Shane faced me. "Everything okay, Ensign?"

"Yeah, everything's fine." I waved a hand. "Just some...personal stuff."

He cocked his head. "Anything you need to discuss?" Didn't take much to read between those lines: *This have anything to do with what we talked about in my office?*

"I'm good." I smiled, and with thoughts of Connor on my mind, it wasn't all that forced. "Don't worry about it."

He eyed me for a moment, then nodded. "Well, if anything changes, you know my door's always open."

"Thanks. I appreciate it."

We continued in opposite directions, and I slipped into my office. I'd barely closed the door when my phone buzzed against my desktop, and I damn near knocked over a chair on my way to grab it.

Sure enough, there was a text from Connor: *Sorry, was in class. Tonight's still good.*

I smiled to myself. Maybe this was a stupid, career-compromising thing to do, but, damn it, I was doing it. No two ways about it—I wanted Connor.

I'm off work at 1600, I texted back. *See you at 1630.*

Chapter Ten
Connor

I'd spent half the day in a private study room at the library on Camp Courtney, which was twenty minutes or so from Kadena. I did actually get some studying done and wrapped up a paper for my economics class, but there was no way around it: my mind was focused on Aiden. When he'd be here. Where we'd go. What we'd do. God, what we'd do...

At a little past four thirty, someone tapped softly on the study room's door, and when I turned around, my heart almost stopped.

There he was. On the other side of the glass, there he was.

As I stood, he opened the door. He slipped inside and closed the door behind him, and for a moment, we just faced each other. My heart definitely wasn't stopped now—it was going ninety miles an hour, blood pounding in my ears as I stared at him like I thought he might suddenly vanish. It had only been twenty-four hours since we'd seen each other, but even with the texts we'd exchanged since then, it had seemed like it was the last time and that was final until just now.

He was here. Really here. A grin slowly spread across his lips, and I realized I was starting to grin myself. We were really here. This was real.

And then he moved, and his lips were against mine, and...and fuck, we were right back in his apartment, up against the wall and out of breath. His body pinned mine to the wall, and his hands kept my hips pressed tight against his. Someone whimpered softly into the kiss, and damn if I knew who it was, but it gave me goose bumps either way.

Abruptly, Aiden broke the kiss. "Crap, sorry." He backed off a little but didn't take his hands off my hips. "We're"—he glanced at the door—"in public."

"Don't care." I kissed him again.

He hesitated for a second but then melted against me. "I missed you last night," he whispered between kisses.

"Missed you too." I broke the kiss and met his eyes. "We should...we should go someplace..."

Aiden nodded. He kissed me lightly, then stepped back. We both glanced at the window. Fortunately, no one was gawking at us. Hopefully no one had noticed us at all.

"Anyplace in particular in mind?" Aiden straightened his clothes as I did the same. "You know this island better than I do."

"Hmm." So hard to think when I was, well, hard. I busied myself collecting my books and papers, taking my time so I had a chance to calm down before we stepped out of the room. "Guess it depends on what you're in the mood for. Going out and checking out the sights, or finding someplace...private."

I glanced at Aiden. His grin told me which option he preferred.

So much for calming down.

I cleared my throat and shuffled some papers. "There's a beach near here. Not too far, but it's really hidden." I turned to him again. "No way in hell anyone'll find it unless they already know it's there."

He spun his keys on his finger, and his grin got bigger. "Show me the way."

We left my car behind. If Dad happened by—and he would—he'd see my car in the library parking lot, and as long as he didn't go wandering inside to find me, I'd be in the clear.

After Aiden had driven us a little ways from the base, I relaxed a bit. We were down a back road now, between sugarcane fields and a row of run-down little shops. No one who saw us out here would give a shit, and anyone who gave a shit would never find us.

I turned to Aiden. "I'm, uh, sorry I didn't tell you about my dad."

"It's okay." He reached across the console and rested his hand on my leg. His palm was warm on my bare skin, and it felt nice. Especially after I'd been so sure he wouldn't want to see me again.

I put my hand over his. "This isn't going to cause you problems at work, is it?"

Aiden scowled but then shook his head. "We had some words this morning, but as long as he doesn't know I'm seeing you..." He glanced at me.

I laughed. "What he doesn't know won't hurt us?"

"Exactly." Aiden clicked his tongue. "And what are the odds? I meet someone here, and his dad's practically my CO."

"The odds are better than you think."

"Yeah?" Another glance at me. "How so?"

"Think about it. The majority of the Americans on this island are military or military dependents. Most of them retire at thirty-eight or forty-two. So when you've got a dependent who's my age, you can bet my dad's been in at least twenty years or so, so he's probably pretty far up the chain, right? And there are only so many people that far up, so the odds are, well... Do the math."

Aiden's brow furrowed. "I hadn't thought about that. But yeah, you're right." He turned toward me and raised an eyebrow. "You a statistics major or something?"

I laughed. "No, but I did take statistics last semester. Guess it shows."

"I'm assuming you passed."

"By the skin of my teeth."

"Really? Sounds like you know it pretty well."

"I do. I was just bored stupid and kind of half-assed a few assignments."

I almost expected a disapproving look, but Aiden just laughed.

"That was me with every math-related class ever invented."

"Seriously?"

He nodded. "I mean, I still got As because I was obsessed with maintaining my GPA so I could go to Annapolis, but, *God*, I was so bored. Science classes, I enjoyed. Even physics and chem were fun. But algebra? Geometry?" He made a face. "I'd rather do extra writing assignments in English."

"Not big on writing?"

"No. Not unless I absolutely have to." He smirked. "So of course I wind up with a job that requires me to *constantly* write up reports."

"Sounds like fun." I wrinkled my nose. "I think I'd jump out the window."

"Yeah, too bad my office is on the first floor."

We both chuckled.

Aiden rested his hand on top of the wheel as he continued down the road. "It's not too bad, though. The meetings with the brass—like, uh, your dad—have their perks. I mean, they're boring as shit and make me want to scratch out my eyes, but the brass has way better coffee than anyone else."

I laughed. "Coffee is the biggest perk of your job?"

"When you're as far down on the totem pole as I am, you take what you can get." He smirked again. "At least in a few years I won't be the one who has to *make* the coffee."

"Now that's ambition."

"You have no idea." He tapped his fingers on the wheel and gestured ahead. "So where am I going?"

I pointed at a narrow street coming up on the left. "That way." I directed him down some back roads, between some more farms and a little cluster of concrete houses. After one tight curve, there were no more houses or farms. Just plants, a couple of Jersey barriers along the abrupt edge of the narrow lane, and ocean. Farther down, the barriers stopped and there was enough shoulder in the shade of a huge banyan tree for Aiden to pull over and park.

As we got out, he paused, leaning on the car door and looking around. "Wow. This really is out in the middle of nowhere."

I grinned over the roof of the car. "That's the idea, isn't it?"

He met my eyes and swallowed hard. "Yeah. It is." I thought his nerves might be getting the best of him, but then he returned my grin as he shut the car door.

The path we followed wasn't much of an actual path. More like a gap between the bushes that was wide enough to walk through. I kept an eye out for snakes—they sometimes hung out in tall grass and thick bushes, and I wasn't big on finding out firsthand if it was true that they'd attack people unprovoked.

At the end of the "path", we found ourselves on a small stretch of beach without another soul in sight. Exactly what I'd hoped for.

Heart beating faster by the second, I turned around to face Aiden. "Well. Here we are."

I thought he might look around, take the whole place in, but he didn't look anywhere except right at me.

"Finally," he whispered and pulled me into his arms. "I was going crazy after you left last night."

"So was I."

He tilted his head, slid a hand around the back of my neck and kissed me. The instant our lips met, every bit of tension in my body melted away. He'd said last night that he still wanted to see me, and I'd hoped to God he wasn't all talk, but kissing was believing. He was here, and this was real. My father's intrusion had given us some speed bumps and some reasons to watch our backs, but at the end of the day, Aiden was here, gently parting my lips and deepening a kiss that was turning my knees to water.

This wasn't the frantic kiss we'd shared at the library or just before my dad crashed our party, but it was hot. Jesus Christ. His tongue gently nudged my lips apart, and he held me close to him as we slowly, lazily explored each other's mouths.

Pulling back, I met his eyes. I reached for his face, but he flinched a little. "Uh. Sorry. I'm—"

"No, it's okay." He gestured at the healing cut above his eyebrow. "It's still tender."

"I wasn't going to touch that part. Promise."

He hesitated but then relaxed. I hesitated too, but when I was sure he was really okay with it, I reached up again. He closed his eyes as my hand drifted across his cheek. The hint of stubble darkening his jaw was rough against my fingertips. His hair was cool under my fingers, and when I curled them slightly, he leaned in and kissed me again.

Fuck, now we were back to where we'd left off last night. Our erections rubbed together through our shorts, and even the humid, tropical air seemed cool compared to the heat of Aiden's body against mine.

Now let's see where this would've gone if we hadn't been interrupted...

My father's intrusion flickered through my mind, and I couldn't help tensing.

"What's wrong?" Aiden asked, barely breaking the kiss.

I pulled back enough to see his eyes. "Are you sure about this?"

"Absolutely." His brow furrowed, and as he touched my face, he whispered, "Are you?"

My mouth had gone dry, so I just nodded.

He inclined his head. "*Are* you?"

"I..." I chewed my lip. "I want to. Bad. But after what happened last night..."

He touched my face. "We both know this won't be easy, and we'll have to lay low, but I don't want to stop. I can deal with your dad. Yeah, he's made some threats to my career, but—"

"What?" My heart dropped. "Shit, I don't want to put your career—"

"He won't know." Aiden ran his fingers through my hair. "But what about you? Will you be okay?"

"Yeah. I'll... He won't kick me out. He knows the only option for me is to go home and live with my mother, and he'd let me hold all-male orgies in our living room before he sent me back to her."

Aiden's eyebrows jumped. "That bad?"

"That bad." I made a gesture like I was tilting a bottle into my mouth.

Aiden grimaced. "Oh. Yeah. Not good."

"No, definitely not."

"He won't kick you out, though, thank God." He took my hand in his and held it between our chests. "As long as you'll be okay, then—"

"But what about you?" I squeezed his hand because I was afraid he was going to get smart and let mine go at any moment. "You said my dad has already threatened you."

Aiden nodded. "Yeah, he did. He threatened to send me to Bahrain or Diego Garcia." He met my eyes. "Let him blow all the smoke he wants." He cupped my cheek with his free hand. "I want to see where this goes. I'm not going anywhere."

"But *is* he blowing smoke?"

Aiden shrugged. "I hope so."

"And if he's not?"

Aiden broke eye contact and didn't speak.

"If you can't do this, I understand." I ran my fingers along his forearm.

"I probably shouldn't." He brought my hand up to his lips. "But I want to. We'll just have to be discreet."

I nodded. "We can do that. There's plenty of places we can go on this island."

For the first time since we'd started this uncomfortable conversation, Aiden smiled. "You'd know better than I would, but I do know there are resorts and hotels all over the island. Hell, there are military lodges on the other bases. Whatever we have to do." He pressed his lips to mine. "We don't even have to sleep together. Just...just for some privacy." Another kiss, longer this time. "So I can have you all to myself for a night."

I shivered. "You have me all to yourself now."

Aiden held me tighter. "And there's always places like this."

I glanced around, wondering when I'd completely forgotten we were standing on a beach with the tide lapping at the sand a few feet away. "This is as good a place as any, isn't it?"

Aiden kissed my forehead. "It's perfect. And there are so many things I want to do with you now that we're here."

"Such as?"

He met my eyes. "How much can you handle?"

"I..." I had no idea. None. Even last night, I hadn't been sure where things would go, only that I didn't want to stop.

"There's no rush." He ran his fingers through my hair. "We can do this a little at a time."

"I have no idea what we're doing," I said. "I just know I don't want to stop."

Aiden leaned in closer. "Then we won't."

Jesus. His kiss. His fucking kiss. Nothing in the world fucked with my ability to think rationally like Aiden's gentle, insistent kiss.

"Why the hell are we standing?" he whispered. "So much more I can do if we're..." He took both my hands, and as he lowered himself onto the sand, he gently tugged me down with him. As he lay back, I started to lie down beside him, but he wrapped an arm around me and pulled me on top of him. The sand was coarse and hot under my knees, but I wouldn't have cared if I were kneeling on pavement. Not with the way Aiden held me close to him and kissed me. One taste of him, and I was too far gone to care about consequences.

He slid a hand over the front of my shorts, and my vision blurred.

"Like that?" he asked between kisses.

"Fuck yeah."

His lips curved against mine. "Thought so."

I might've had a witty response to that, but it disappeared when Aiden started on my zipper. I suddenly couldn't even remember how to form words. Somehow my lips knew how to respond to his and kept moving and teasing him back when he teased me, but my brain went blank and the world spun around me as he undid my shorts.

And then his palm was against my dick. Even kissing went out the window right then.

"Shit..."

"You okay?" He sounded playful, like he knew damn well I was *just* fine.

"Uh-huh."

He laughed softly. As he fidgeted under me, it took me a second to figure out what he was doing. Then I realized he was unbuttoning and unzipping his own shorts. Oh God. Oh my fucking God. *Please, please, don't let anything interrupt this...*

Aiden wrapped his fingers around both our cocks and damn near blew my mind. The underside of his cock was against the underside of mine. It was weird, having another guy's dick this close to mine. And, God, he was hard. Easily as hard as I was. Knowing I turned him on... Fuck, what a rush.

Without even thinking about it, I rubbed my cock against his.

Aiden's breath caught. "Holy shit."

I hesitated. "Is this okay?"

He nodded. "Yeah." He put his other hand on my hips and encouraged me to move, pressing against me and stroking us both as I fucked his fist. "Keep...keep doing that."

I kept doing that. I'd never felt anything like this. I had no idea what I was doing, only that my body wanted to move like this, and Aiden kept egging me on, and if we did this much longer I was going to come. Fuck, just being against Aiden was going to get me off, but the way we moved together, cocks rubbing against each other like this, I was going to lose my fucking mind.

"That feel good?" he asked.

"Mm-hmm." I kissed him but kept running out of air. I moved faster, and he moved too, and, Jesus, he knew exactly how to move to turn "feels good" into "oh my God". I tried to imagine how this would feel if his cock were inside me—or mine were inside him—but I couldn't hold on to any thoughts at all besides how good it felt right then, skin rubbing skin and bodies moving together like they knew how to do this even when my mind was completely useless.

Aiden broke the kiss with a gasp. His eyes flew open and his back arched. He thrust against me harder, the friction making my eyes water and pushing me closer and closer to what was absolutely going to be an amazing orgasm.

He groaned softly and shuddered. "Holy...*fuck.*"

And just like that, I came. I thrust hard against him, not even caring if it hurt, because, Jesus Christ, the only thing that mattered was fucking against him, thrusting, pumping, keeping my orgasm going as long as possible. Aiden whimpered, and he was fucking against me too, his semen mixed with mine between us.

I relaxed. Then he did. Our foreheads touched, and we both panted.

"That was hot," he murmured.

"Mm-hmm." I licked my lips, the tip of my tongue brushing his and making both of us shiver. "If it's this good now..."

Aiden's lips curved into a grin, and he kissed me. "Just say the word, and I will fuck you until you can't walk."

Another shudder went through me. "Promise?"

Aiden kissed me again. "Promise."

Chapter Eleven
Aiden

I paced beside my car in the parking lot outside the shopping center down the street from my apartment.

This was a bad idea. A stupid one. Just like every time Connor and I had sneaked off to a beach or a restaurant or wherever over the last couple of weeks. We'd seen each other almost every day since we'd agreed to fly below his father's radar, and I had the same ball of nerves in my gut every single time. The same certainty that we were going to get caught, that we were idiots, that I should really just tell him this was a bad idea and go our separate ways. Just call it quits before General Bradshaw made mincemeat of my career.

But that ball of nerves turned into something entirely different the instant Connor's car came into view. As it always was, just seeing that brown Nissan was enough to make my heart flutter, and when he stepped out of the driver's side, I couldn't help smiling. What was left of my good sense went out the window as he came closer.

Yep, this was a bad idea. And nope, I wasn't bailing on it. If anything, I was tempted to suggest we stay at my apartment for a few hours like we'd done a couple of times, but Connor had said he'd thought of a great place to spend this afternoon.

We exchanged glances as he stopped in front of me. Much as I wanted to kiss him, that wasn't a good idea, and I at least had the presence of mind to not push my luck. For one, we'd never get out of this parking lot and neither of us had a backseat big enough to avoid some serious neck and back pain.

For another, well, we were still a little too close to a base full of people who might recognize either of us.

Hooking my thumbs in my pockets to keep from reaching for him, I said, "So what adventure do you have planned for us today?"

Connor's hands mirrored mine. "I was thinking we could check out Nakijin Castle."

"Another castle?"

"There's a bunch of them."

"How long's the drive?"

"Pretty long."

"Awesome. Let's go."

I loved the long drives. We'd explored all kinds of places, and my favorites were the more remote ones. They were usually cool in their own right, but spending an hour or two in the car with Connor, just cruising through villages and winding coastal roads, was the best.

Nakijin Castle was on the west side of the island, half an hour or so east of Nago. We wound through some sugarcane fields, a couple of villages and some stretches that were shaded by a thick canopy of trees, before the signs finally guided us into a parking lot beside a small visitor center. We paid the entry fee—just a few bucks—and headed up to the castle.

The castle was high up on a hill overlooking the East China Sea. I wasn't sure if the walls had been rebuilt or if they were still intact from the fourteenth century, but the structure was pretty fucking impressive. I'd only seen two other castles so far—Katsuren with Connor earlier this week and Nakagusuku from a distance—and they were all pretty cool. Huge stone walls, foundations from buildings that were there in the fourteenth century—they were so fascinating I almost ran into three spiderwebs. Which wouldn't have been all that unusual or startling if not for the fact that the webs were bigger than bicycle wheels and their occupants the size of my hand.

"Jesus Christ." I stumbled back from damn near getting acquainted with one of the black-and-yellow spiders. "Those things are huge!"

Connor laughed. "Just be glad they're not poisonous. They're about the only thing on this island that aren't."

"Well. That's good." I eyed the thing, trying not to think about how many I'd passed without even knowing it, especially en route to Hiji Falls. "Looks like they can still bite, though."

"Of course they can. And it'd probably hurt like hell."

"Ya think? I'll keep my hands—holy fuck. Does that one have a cicada in its web?"

Connor craned his neck. "Yeah, looks like it does."

"Oh my God." The insect was the size of my thumb and was probably little more than an appetizer for that...that...*thing*.

Something brushed the back of my neck, and I made a sound I'm not even a little bit proud of as I tried to smack the thing away.

Connor laughed so hard he doubled over.

Still swiping at my neck, I glared at him. "Asshole."

He batted his eyes. "What? I didn't know you were an arachnophobe."

"You learn something new every day," I grumbled.

Resting a hand on my hip, he kissed me. "You're adorable when you're—"

"Shut up." I laughed, playfully pushing him away. He chuckled, and I drew him back in for a longer kiss. "You're a pain in the ass, you know that?"

"Are you complaining?"

"Not at all."

We wandered around the castle for a while, checking out the walls and gardens. There weren't a lot of people around, fortunately. Just a few Japanese tourists. Not a single American in sight, which meant not a single person who might recognize either of us. The more we walked around, the more I relaxed, letting myself enjoy being with Connor and not sweating bullets over getting caught.

Down below the castle was a big enclosure that resembled a horse pasture. Just some grass on a slope surrounded by the high rock wall. As we walked around that enclosure along the foot of the castle, I said, "Think your dad suspects anything? That you're out with me?"

Connor laughed. "Nah. He's used to me taking off for hours at a time. Especially when I'm pissed off, and believe me, he *knows* I'm pissed off."

"I assume that means he hasn't followed you again?"

"Not that I know of. I think he fully expects me to go behind his back and see you, but he's probably pretty sure he scared you enough you'll avoid me like the plague."

My stomach started to knot again. If I had an ounce of common sense, I *would* avoid Connor like the plague, but all that common sense went straight out the window any time he looked at me or touched me.

Connor stopped walking. I did too, and as I faced him, he touched my arm.

"I don't want to fuck up your career," he said. "If you can't do this, just say so."

"As long as we're discreet, we'll be okay." I brought his hand up to my lips. "Don't sweat it."

"But you have to work with my dad."

"And you have to live with him."

He grimaced. "Don't remind me."

I kissed his forehead. "We'll be fine. We can do this without him catching on."

"Just say so if you don't think—"

I stopped him with a soft kiss. "Let's not go there. I want to be here with you, and I couldn't care less what your dad thinks."

He searched my eyes for a moment, then smiled. "I couldn't care less either."

"Good."

We continued wandering around the enclosure and then headed back up into the castle and all the way to the uppermost enclosure. From here, there was a 360-degree view of this part of the island—clusters of concrete houses, huge expanses of green forests, a patchwork of farms, highways and, of course, the ocean. I could imagine a king standing up here centuries ago, looking out at the land and the ocean.

"Can you imagine living in this place?" I mused. "Back when it was an actual castle, I mean."

"Hell yeah." With a smirk, he stretched out his arms. "Everything the light touches would be *mine!*"

I laughed. "It'd all be yours. The entire tree-covered rock."

He shrugged. "Shit, I'd take it."

"You and me both. Not sure I'd want the mortgage, though."

"If you're a king, you don't have a mortgage. You just take it from the other guy."

"Good point." Craning my neck, I leaned out to look down at the forest below. A stone shifted under my foot. I flailed and instinctively reached for Connor, and he caught my arm.

"You okay?" he asked.

"Yeah." I regained my footing without losing too much more of my dignity. "Just need to watch where I'm putting my feet, apparently."

"Good idea." He loosened his grasp on my arm, and let his hand slide down until it found mine. Our fingers slipped between each other's, and it felt perfectly normal.

As we walked on, he glanced at the sky. "We probably should make our way back to the parking lot. The sun'll be going down soon."

I shrugged. "We've got time."

He glanced at me, and I stopped. "I'm not in any hurry," I said. "Not unless you are."

"Absolutely not. Just don't want you to get bored when we can't actually see anything."

"I won't get bored. I just like being here." I touched his face. "With you."

Connor held my gaze. "Me too."

I started to pull him closer, but he resisted. Didn't pull away completely, just didn't let himself be drawn all the way in.

"What's wrong?"

He swallowed. "This is... You're okay with this?" He swept his tongue across his lips. "In public?"

"Yes." I ran my thumb along his cheekbone. "I don't care who knows."

Connor relaxed as he said, "Neither do I."

I wrapped my arms around him and didn't care if anyone saw us. His kiss was so gentle and perfect I didn't care about anything except tasting it. Tasting him. So what if I got a hard-on? I was lucky I didn't get one just being next to him, so there was no point in denying myself a long, amazing kiss.

He pulled back enough to meet my eyes but then glanced to the side and did a double take. "Wow."

"Hmm?" I followed his gaze, and...yeah. Wow.

The sun was inching into the water, and the sky had turned red, orange and purple. From up here, the view was incredible, just like it had been at Cape Hedo. We watched in silence, still holding on to each other.

When the sun had set, I met his eyes again. The warm wind had ruffled his hair a little, and I brushed a few stray strands out of his face. "Guess we should get back to the cars while we still have enough light."

"Yeah. Except I don't really want to leave."

"Neither do I, but..." I released him. "We'll just have to come back up. Isn't like it's going anywhere."

Connor slipped his hand into mine. "Let's go."

We exchanged smiles, and then, hand in hand, we slowly made our way back toward the parking lot in the fading daylight. As the cars came into view, Connor looked at his watch and sighed. "By the time we get back, I'll have to head home, or my dad will ask questions. Which means we can't..."

"Connor." I skimmed his jaw with the backs of my fingers. "If I was worried about that, we'd have left a long time ago."

He searched my eyes for a moment but then relaxed. "We should do this again soon."

"Absolutely. The sooner the better."

We continued toward our cars. In the back of my mind, I was disappointed that we were going our separate ways instead of finding a flat surface and some condoms, but I could be patient. Of course I wanted him, and there was no way I'd get any sleep until I'd jerked off at least once, but I couldn't even bring myself to feel too badly about the fact that I wouldn't have him tonight. Because I'd see him tomorrow. And the next day. And if we both played our cards right, maybe the day after that.

I barely knew him, but he did something to me that no other man had. I couldn't even put my finger on what that was. All I knew was my world had been off its axis since the moment I'd laid eyes on him at Hiji Falls.

And I didn't want it back on that axis any time soon.

Chapter Twelve
Connor

I dropped Aiden off at his car, and after a long, long kiss—one that almost convinced me to say *the hell with it, let's go back to your apartment*—headed home.

I was... I didn't even know how I felt. Turned on? Giddy? Frustrated that we were going our separate ways for the night? Stupidly excited that I was going to see him tomorrow? Fuck. I was all over the place. And I could barely remember a thing about Nakijin. From this trip, anyway. I'd been up there a few times on my own, so I had a solid mental picture of everything, but tonight all I could remember was Aiden.

This was crazy. We'd been dating, what, three weeks now? And even after that shit with my father, he kept coming back for more. And I wanted more. How much more? Hell if I knew. I just knew I didn't want this to stop.

We kept seeing each other, which meant coming up with creative excuses for being out of the house. Fortunately, I was rarely home anyway, so even though my dad still gave me The Look sometimes when I left, he and my stepmother didn't seem to suspect a thing.

A week or so after we visited Nakijin, Aiden met me at the library after work.

"I haven't eaten all day," he said. "Do you mind if we stop for something to eat?"

"Not at all. I'm pretty hungry myself." I did a quick rundown of the places I knew in this area. "You like curry?"

"Like Indian food?"

"Well, kind of. But this is Japanese curry."

He glanced at me. "What's the difference?"

My jaw dropped. "You've never had Japanese curry? Seriously?"

"It's not all that common in Nevada or Maryland, if you hadn't noticed."

"But you've been on the island for a few weeks."

I sighed dramatically. "I know. I've failed at being an American on Okinawa."

"You totally have." He pulled into the parking lot of what looked like a fast-food joint, though most of the signage was in Japanese. I didn't even know what most of it said—I could speak a little Japanese, but hell if I could read more than five or six Kanji characters. All I knew was this place had *awesome* food.

On the way in, Aiden said, "So this is Japanese curry? How is it different from Indian curry?"

"The spice is a bit milder," I said. "And the flavor's stronger. I like it better, personally. Indian food's okay, but this stuff is amazing." I took in a deep breath as we stepped through the front door. "It even smells amazing."

Aiden sniffed the air. "You're right, it does. Hell yeah, I'll try it."

A waitress seated us and took our drink orders.

The menus were pretty straightforward. Most of the curry dishes had some sort of meat or vegetable over rice with curry on top.

Aiden looked at me over his menu. "So what do you recommend for the heat level?"

"I'd order a two or a three tops."

"Two or three?" He snorted. "I can handle more—"

"*Trust* me."

He arched his recently healed eyebrow but then shrugged. When the waitress returned, he ordered first.

"I'll take the chicken curry." He gestured at the menu.

"And the spice?" she asked.

Aiden glanced at me, then looked up at her again. "Two."

"Two." She looked at me. "And you?"

"Same thing," I said. "But make the spice a one."

She nodded, then read off the order, making sure everything was correct before she headed back to the kitchen.

"Only one?" Aiden grinned as the waitress walked away. "And you're telling me I should rein it back to two or three?"

I shrugged. "I can handle more. I just like to taste my food."

"Fair enough. I like it hot, but I do like to taste it too."

"So you're not one of those guys who tries to show off by eating hot stuff?"

Aiden laughed. "No, not me. I got that out of my system at the Academy. When you start drinking Tabasco and Sriracha sauces just to prove you've got the balls to do it..." He wrinkled his nose and shook his head.

My mouth fell open. "You *drank* that stuff?"

"Unfortunately."

"What is it with Navy guys and hot shit?"

"Hey!" He glared at me but couldn't hide a smirk. "What's that supposed to mean?"

"It means every time I hear about stupid people and hot food, there's some Navy guy involved."

Aiden snorted. "For some reason, that really doesn't surprise me. Us or the Marines, anyway."

I chuckled. "Yeah, well, one time the rear admiral was here, and someone had told him the curry was awesome. So my dad and some of the other guys brought him here." I laughed and shook my head. "Fucker thought he could handle a ten."

"I'm guessing that didn't work out so well?"

"Oh my God, no." I couldn't help snickering at the memory of my dad telling this story. "They won't let you order above a five until you've proven you can handle a five, but someone ordered a ten for him."

Aiden's eyes widened. "What happened?"

"According to my dad? The guy finished it, but he was sniffling like a baby the entire time."

"But he finished it anyway?"

"Of course he did." I rolled my eyes. "You don't just puss out in front of your underlings."

Aiden laughed. "Wow, I would have paid to see that."

"Me too. My dad told me about it, but I wasn't there."

"Too funny," he said.

Our food showed up a moment later—this place was lightning fast—and we in silence for a couple of minutes. As he turned his head to glance at something, the scar on his eyebrow caught my eye. The stitches had come out a while ago, and now there was just a jagged pink line cutting through his eyebrow. It wasn't super obvious, but it was definitely visible.

Picking at my curry, I said, "I'm curious about something. And you, uh, you don't have to answer."

Aiden arched his unscarred eyebrow. "Go ahead."

"I was on your Facebook profile last night, and I noticed you had pictures of..." I gestured at my own eyebrow.

Immediately, his face colored, and he broke eye contact. "Right."

"You said that happened up at Hiji Falls." I hesitated, not wanting to pry. "But you had stitches when I met you, and that was the first time you'd been up there."

Aiden swallowed. "It's, uh, it's kind of a long story." He met my eyes, and I swore his begged me not to press the issue, no matter how insanely curious I was.

So I just shrugged. "Okay. I was just wondering."

He smiled, and his whole body seemed more relaxed now, like he really thought I'd push for an answer. Then he cleared his throat. "So, uh, I know I just completely evaded your question, but I'm curious about something too."

Well, at least it was a subject change. "Shoot."

"Why haven't you dated anyone before?"

So much for the topic being less awkward than the cut over his eyebrow. I lowered my gaze, wishing I could blame the warmth in my face on the heat of the day. "I..."

"You don't have to answer." He reached across the table and touched my arm. "I didn't answer your question. You sure don't have to answer mine."

I met his eyes. "Honestly? It's really hard to find a guy when you're the general's kid."

Aiden grimaced. "Oh. Yeah. I can imagine."

"Even when I was in high school, guys were weird about it. They always say the senior officers' kids are untouchable if you know what's good for you." I rolled my eyes. "It's tough, you know? *Everyone* knows who my dad is. That's why I wasn't exactly forthcoming about him when I met you."

"I never even thought about that."

I dragged a forkful of rice through the curry sauce, saturating it as much as I could. "I've never been able to get away from it. I was in DOD schools my entire life from middle school on. And here, I'm pretty isolated."

Aiden whistled. "Wow, yeah. I guess that would make it difficult." He paused. "I'm surprised you don't hang out with the locals."

"My Japanese isn't that good." I laughed. "If I'd known I was staying here past high school, I'd have learned a bit more."

"So you're stuck here. With your dad."

"Yep. I was seriously looking forward to getting out on my own after graduation, but..." I shook my head. "Just wasn't in the cards. Not until I finish my degree."

"That's gotta be rough." Aiden watched me for a moment. "Out of curiosity, how *does* your dad feel? About you being gay. Not being with me."

I took a bite of curry-covered rice and washed it down with my soda. "Dad's been great about it. He just doesn't like me dating military guys. And, well, there aren't a lot of Americans on this island anyway, let alone civilians. I don't speak enough Japanese to connect very well with one of the local nationals." I shook my head. "So, the pickings have been a little slim, you know?"

"Believe me, I get it." He rested his arm on the edge of the table. "Your dad's cool with it, though? He's not homophobic?"

"Not at all. You should've heard him when people were fighting to keep DADT in place. I think he almost punched out an admiral over it."

Aiden laughed. "You're kidding."

"Nope."

"Well, that's good. Your parents are supportive, so—"

"My dad is supportive," I said. "Not my parents."

"Oh really?"

I nodded. "I came out when I was in junior high. While I was still living with my mom in San Diego."

"And that...didn't go well?"

"No. She lost her fucking mind. I was scared to death about what my dad would do, but I guess I thought my mom would be okay with it. I mean, I waited until she was sober to tell her. She's usually sane before she hits the bottle."

"But she wasn't that time?"

I whistled. "No. Not at all. Flipped out completely." My mind went back to that day, and I couldn't help shuddering. "You would've thought I'd just told her I had bodies hidden in my closet, not that I was coming out of it, you know? And then when she tried to put me into straight camp, I—"

"Straight camp?" Aiden almost choked. "Sorry, sorry, I don't mean to interrupt, but...*straight camp*? Seriously?"

I nodded. "And it was one of the ones that got shut down a couple of years ago for beating kids too." I shuddered again, this time at the memory of how close I'd come to setting foot in that awful place.

Aiden stared at me. "My God. Did you go?"

"No. I got in touch with my dad and told him everything. He told me go to my grandma's house, and three days later, he was there to get me."

"Wow. Did your mom fight him?"

"She tried, but Dad threatened to have her hemmed up for child abuse and let her commanding officer know she'd started drinking again."

Aiden blinked. "Holy shit."

"Needless to say, she let it go. She still tries to persuade me to come home and live with her, but..." I shook my head.

"Good call," he said quietly.

"So anyway, I've been here since then, and once I got out of high school, all that was left were guys stationed here." I sighed and rolled my eyes. "Just *try* finding one who'll admit he's gay."

Aiden grimaced. "I can relate, believe me."

"And even if he does, the second he finds out who my dad is..."

A little bit of color bloomed in Aiden's cheeks. "I know that feeling."

"Sorry."

"Don't be. I wouldn't be here if I didn't think you were worth it." He winked, which did all kinds of crazy shit to my heart rate.

I cleared my throat. "So what about you? Being gay in the military and all?"

"Not as bad as it used to be since DADT was lifted, but it's still a political issue. I haven't been out in the Fleet long enough to really have a feel for that, but at the Academy, it was tricky to figure out who was gay and would keep his mouth shut. At least I could leave the base and hook up with civilians, though."

"Must be nice," I muttered. "Damn, I guess I should've unloaded my virginity while I was in high school."

"Why's that?"

"Because fumbling through it with some other teenager beats the hell out of being twenty and still a virgin on an island where I can't sleep with anyone my age who speaks my language."

"I wouldn't be so sure about that."

Which part? Because you speak my language...

I gulped, wondering when they'd turned off the AC in this place. "Yeah?"

"Yep. Listen, you're obviously in a tough spot. I think you can be forgiven for being cautious about things and not hooking up with anyone till now." Aiden smiled. "And if it means you never have to fumble through it with some other teenager..." He let his grimace finish the thought. "Just call it a bonus. Trust me."

"Speaking from experience?"

Aiden nodded. "Unfortunately."

"Maybe I did dodge a bullet, then."

"You have no idea."

"I guess not." I chased a grain of rice through the curry still on my plate. "So what about your family? Do they know you're gay?"

Aiden nodded. "They figured it out before I did, actually."

"Seriously?"

"Yep. And they were fine with it, except my dad was absolutely scared shitless I was going to get beaten up at school." Aiden sipped his soda. "So he enrolled me in every martial arts and self-defense course he could find. Which turned out to be a good thing, I guess."

I sat up straighter. "Ooh, you're into martial arts?"

"Yep. It came in handy when some guys tried to jerk me around, and I enjoyed it a lot." Something in his expression faltered a little, his gaze dropping. "I'm a bit out of practice. I've got two black belts and won a whole bunch of shit when I was in high school, but..." He shook his head. "It kind of fell by the wayside while I was at the Academy. I'm hoping to pick it up again, though." With a forced smile, he added, "You never know when something like that might come in handy."

An awkward silence set in, so I said, "Well, there are places on base and out in town. This is Okinawa, after all."

"Might have to check it out. You ever thought about doing it?"

"I have, but..." I shrugged. "Never quite got around to it."

"You should try it." He smiled a bit more genuinely. "It's fun."

"Well, if you like getting thrown around by other men, right?"

"Yeah." He winked. "And who doesn't like that?"

I just shivered.

"So." He pushed his plate away and took a drink. "We've got all evening. Where to?"

"Well..." I checked my watch. We still had tons of daylight left. "We could go check out the lighthouse at Cape Zanpa. It's not far from here, and it's as good a place as any to walk off all this food."

"Let's go."

Chapter Thirteen
Aiden

We got used to sneaking around. Connor was a pro at flying below his father's radar, and as near as I could tell, Bradshaw didn't suspect a thing. I could look him in the eye at work without flinching, even knowing I'd be out with Connor in a matter of hours.

The secrecy added a little thrill to it, but it wasn't as addictive as Connor himself. As soon as I was off work each day, I'd hurry back to my apartment, throw on some civvies, and pick him up wherever we'd agreed to meet. Then we were off to wherever we could go and not run into any Americans, especially those from my command or who knew the Bradshaw family.

We were all over the island. North end. South end. Snorkeling. Checking out the castles. We stayed away from the bases and from Gate Two Street—too many people who might recognize either of us, and after my encounter with that asshole Marine, I was content to stay the fuck away from Gate Two Street anyway.

I was happy like this. We still fooled around whenever we had the chance—especially on a secluded beach or when we dared sneak back to my apartment—but mostly we just spent hours on end together. We watched more than a few sunsets while wandering around a beach. Or the ruins of another old castle. Or driving aimlessly around the island, checking out the remotest parts to see what was out there. Or having dinner in a restaurant in the middle of nowhere with a menu we couldn't begin to read. Or grabbing a bite at the Family Mart before taking off to some deserted beach.

Or, as we were tonight, lying on our backs on the short, coarse grass near the lip of a cliff at Cape Manzamo.

A few hours ago, we'd had a spectacular view of the ocean and the coastline, but now there was nothing to see but stars. There wasn't a soul around. The park was technically closed and had been since sundown, which was almost two hours ago, but no one had tried to kick us out, so we didn't move.

We were fully dressed. We'd walked out here hand in hand, and we'd paused for the odd kiss, but lying here like this wasn't the aftermath of some dangerously public interlude. Connor's fingers laced loosely between mine, his thumb running back and forth as if he just wanted to stay constantly aware of that soft, warm contact.

As the sky darkened, more stars came out. Not just the bright ones you could see in the cities, but the tiny, faint ones that were almost impossible to see with any light pollution at all.

"This is one thing I miss about living in Nevada." I pointed upward. "Skies like that."

"Yeah? Even near Vegas?"

"Well, you had to drive away from the city, of course, but get an hour or so away on a clear night and it's fucking amazing." I paused. "Cold as shit, but so worth it."

"Cold? In the desert?"

"At night, you'd better believe it."

"Huh."

We fell silent again. After a while, Connor released my hand and shifted beside me. I started to ask if he was comfortable, but then I realized he was moving closer. I wrapped my arm around his shoulders as he rested his head on my chest, and our fingers were once again laced together, this time on his arm.

We didn't talk for a while. It wasn't awkward, though. I'd learned to enjoy these moments when we just enjoyed each other's company and the scenery. It didn't matter if we were lost in a conversation or just lying together in silence—I liked being with him. Period.

Beside me, Connor shifted again.

"Comfortable?" I asked.

"Yeah. Just, uh, thinking."

"About?"

He didn't answer immediately. "About, uh..." He paused. "I've kind of been thinking the last few days. About how far we've..." Another pause, and this time he cleared his throat and shifted again. "How far we haven't gone, I guess."

"Yeah?" I absently stroked his hair.

"The thing is, I...want to."

There was no way in hell he didn't feel me shiver. I moistened my lips. "You do?"

Connor nodded, his face brushing my shirt. "I'm just..."

"Nervous?"

"Very. I know I...I know I want to." He rubbed his thumb along the side of my finger. "Just really nervous."

"Everyone's nervous their first time." I kissed the top of his head. "If they say otherwise, they're lying."

He laughed softly. "Guess I'm in good company."

"You are. Definitely."

"Does it, uh, hurt?"

"It can." I let go of his hand and ran mine up and down his arm. "Depending on how careful your partner is."

"Oh."

"And it definitely doesn't hurt if you're on top."

His fingers twitched between mine. "I guess it wouldn't, would it?"

"Nope." Still stroking his arm, I thought back to my own apprehension about anal sex. How all the horror stories and fears had stacked up against the real thing. "Listen, if we get there—and I want to, but I'm not in any hurry—we'll be careful and take it slow." I kissed the top of his head again. "I promise."

Connor relaxed a little, but he was still tense.

I gently freed my arm and turned onto my side, propping myself up on my elbow and meeting his eyes in the near darkness. "Have you ever done, um, anything on your own?" I paused. "Like with a toy?"

"A dildo?"

"Yeah."

He nodded.

"Did you like it?"

"Once I figured out how much lube was enough, yeah."

I trailed the backs of my fingers down his face. "So you know it can be done, right? And you can handle it?"

"Yeah, I guess I do."

"That's a damned good start." I leaned down and kissed him gently. "And even if you hadn't tried it yourself, I promise you, I'll make sure it's not painful for you."

"Thank you," he whispered and pulled me down into a longer kiss.

My stomach fluttered as we held each other on the grass beneath the stars. I was nervous too, because I wanted to make sure things went right with him. I wanted to protect him. I wanted to have him. I wanted everything between us—the sex, everything—to be perfect. More than ever before with any other guy, I wanted—needed—this to be right.

Connor was nervous about the prospect of having sex with me. This was all uncharted territory for him, from the first touch to wherever we eventually took things. It was all new and probably scared the hell out of him.

Me? I'd been there, done that, but he'd have been blown away if he knew how nervous I was. Not about the physical aspect. No, I could handle that. Sex with him would probably kill me if everything else had been any indication, but what a way to go. Still, that wasn't what had me on pins and needles with butterflies in my stomach and all that crap.

This wasn't just about the sex we hadn't had yet, or the fooling around we had done. If what we were doing was just about sex, we'd hide his car somewhere and spend every waking hour in my bed. Or these long drives would be to the resort hotels up near Nago, or the more cosmopolitan ones down in Naha.

But we didn't hide.

Yeah, we fooled around sometimes, but we spent more time out of bed than in it. And I liked it. I liked the time we spent together, whether we were making out or going out, and that was the part that scared me. Connor may have been uneasy about taking the next step in the bedroom, but I was a nervous wreck over the places this was going that didn't involve our bodies.

The car bounced and bumped through massive potholes as he drove between a couple of sugarcane fields.

"You sure we're not going to get lost back here?" I asked.

Connor laughed. "We're on an island the size of a potato chip crumb. How lost can we get?"

"Fair enough. But..." I looked around at the sugarcane fields and forest around us. As the fields ended, and this barely existent road was the only evidence of civilization, I glanced at Connor again. "Okay, let me rephrase. Do you know where we're going?"

"We're going until we run out of road."

"And when we get there?"

The car bounced through another pothole. As the road leveled out—sort of—he glanced at me. "Then we'll be at a beach."

"Will we?"

"Probably." He put a hand on my thigh. "We've done this how many times before? Trust me on this."

"Mm-hmm." I would've taken his hand but didn't want to take my own off the wheel on this bumpy "road". "One of these days, you're going to steer me into a pit full of spiders, I swear."

He laughed and patted my leg. "I'm not crazy about spiders either. I promise, that won't happen. And I'll bet good money that this road"—he gestured up ahead—"takes us to a beach."

It was a good thing I didn't bet against him. After another click or so, we ran out of road, and, sure enough, there was a gorgeous expanse of beach without a single soul in sight.

"Ready to do some snorkeling?" he asked.

"Absolutely." We'd been in the water a couple of times, but today was perfect for it. The water was glass smooth and crystal clear, especially in this secluded little lagoon.

"I checked online," Connor said as we got out of the car. "There aren't any jellyfish swarms out here right now. Closest one was spotted like ten kilometers from here."

"That's good." I popped the trunk. "I really don't feel like tangling with one of those bastards today."

"No shit." He shuddered. "I like box jellyfish about as well as you like spiders."

"Great." I pulled his snorkel bag out and handed it to him. "I've got the land covered, you've got the water. Between us, we're fucked."

He hoisted the bag onto his shoulder. "Just be glad neither of us is weird about snakes."

"No kidding. Though, quite honestly, I'd rather tangle with the snakes in the water than on land."

"Yeah, me too. If the Habu learn to swim, we're all fucked."

I shuddered. Snorkeling around deadly snakes was mildly unnerving, but at least the sea snakes weren't aggressive. The Habu were nasty motherfuckers. If I ever saw one of them in the water, that'd be my last swim. Ever.

With our snorkel bags on our shoulders, I locked up the car, and we picked our way down the rocks to the beach.

The beach that turned out to be spectacular. Part flat, weathered rock. Part gleaming white sand. The water was calm and smooth, even in the open water beyond the mouth of the lagoon.

"Is it deep enough to swim here?" I asked.

"Should be." Connor shrugged. "If it's not, we'll walk out until it is."

"Fair enough."

A rocky outcropping provided plenty of shade, so we put our stuff down under that. We changed into our swim trunks—the water was warm enough, we didn't bother with wet suits—and put on some sunscreen.

As I covered my neck and shoulders in SPF 50, I looked around. We were absolutely alone. There wasn't a soul in sight, not even a ship or a fishing boat out in the water.

No one in the world knew we were here. And since it was a Saturday, we had hours to ourselves before either of us needed to be anywhere.

I slowly turned to Connor.

He'd been smoothing some sunscreen on his arms when he met my eyes. After a moment, his hand stopped. Something like excitement or maybe nerves lifted his eyebrows. "What?"

"What?"

"You're looking at me like..."

I grinned. "Like what?"

"Like that."

I couldn't even think of anything witty to say, or anything flirty, or anything at all. Because I was looking at him like that, and the only thing wrong with this moment was the fact that I wasn't touching him.

I fixed that in a hurry.

Connor didn't resist. As I pulled him into my arms, he raised his chin and met me in a hungry kiss, and he was already getting hard in his swim trunks.

"You know," I murmured between kisses, "we have this whole beach to ourselves."

His lips curved against mine. "We do. What should we do with it?"

I didn't answer. I just wrapped my arms around him, shifted my weight and lowered us both onto the sand. Even in the shade, the sand was hot against my bare skin, but Connor's body was even hotter. And if he kept kissing me like that, mine was going to burst into flames.

I pulled his head back and kissed his neck, not giving a damn about the faint taste and scent of sunscreen.

Connor groaned, his voice thrumming against my lips. "We're never going to make it into the water like this."

"I don't care." I dragged my lips across his collarbone. "Do you?"

"Not at all." Arching against me, he asked, "You ever had sex on the beach?"

"No." I came up to kiss him again, letting it linger for a moment. "But there's a first time for everything."

Connor tensed.

I stroked his face. "Relax. Doesn't have to be today."

"What if I want it to be today?"

Shivering, I leaned down and kissed him again. "We don't have any lube or condoms with us."

"Damn it."

"It's okay. We'll get there."

Truth was, I did have lube and condoms with me. Plenty of them. But I wasn't ready to take Connor there yet. Not until I was sure he was ready.

"We should lose the swim trunks," he murmured. "They're getting in the way."

"They really are."

We tossed our swimming trunks on top of the rest of our gear, and then laid a towel down on the sand. It was cooler against my back than the sand had been, and less gritty, but I didn't care either way as long as Connor's hot—and now naked, oh my God—body was against mine.

I wrapped my arms around him and let myself get completely lost in the soft but undeniably hungry way he kissed. His tongue explored my mouth, but he was never forceful, never overbearing. He struck the most endearing balance between curious and cautious—trying new things and seeking out more, but still picking up on my cues and responding to them without resistance.

And although he may have been a virgin, his body sure knew what to do. His hips moved against mine, rubbing the underside of his cock against the underside of mine, and our breathing fell into perfect sync.

He broke the kiss with a gasp. "Oh my God…"

"Like that?"

"Mm-hmm." He let his lips graze mine. "You?"

"Fuck yeah." I pulled him down into another kiss. "And there's no hurry for more. I've done all this before. This is all at your speed. Whatever you're ready for, say the word."

"I think I'm *finally* ready for this part." He kissed the middle of my sternum, and planted one light kiss after another on my skin, each one a little lower than the last. My abs contracted under his soft lips, and I released a shuddering breath as he flicked his tongue across my skin.

"Jesus…"

He looked up at me, eyes gleaming, and flicked his tongue again. I gasped and squirmed—that area wasn't particularly erogenous, but just knowing his mouth was on me was enough to turn me inside out. Knowing he was heading lower…

I moaned as he kissed my stomach again. Then he continued downward. The gentle, tentative kisses he trailed along my hip bone were almost more than I could take. Fuck. I was coming unglued, and he hadn't even touched my cock.

He trailed more soft kisses along my hip bone. Whether it was to tease me or psych himself up, I had no idea, but it was a hell of a turn-on. Holding myself up on my elbows, I could barely focus my eyes as I watched him inch closer and closer to my very erect cock. I knew what that mouth was capable of when he kissed—I had to feel him give a blowjob.

Connor looked up at me. He grinned again, this time nervously, and I returned it. I ran my fingers through his hair, and then along his cheek, and when I dragged my thumb across his lower lip, he shivered. I slipped my thumb into his mouth, and he immediately closed his lips around it. His tongue teased it in a pantomime of what I hoped—oh sweet Jesus, I hoped—he was about to do to my cock.

"You don't have to." I withdrew my thumb and slid it back into his mouth. "But don't let me stop you if you want to."

He grinned around my thumb. Then he ran his tongue along it before pulling free and dipping his head, leaving my hand hovering in the air as he slowly—maybe cautiously—ran his tongue around the head of my cock.

"Oh. Fuck." My hand still hovered, though it shook a little now, but I couldn't decide between resting it in his hair or just dropping it to my side. It was too damned hard to think about anything, even something that simple, when Connor's tongue was on my dick. Finally, I settled on grabbing a fistful of the towel under me just for something to hold on to.

Steadying my cock with one hand around the base, Connor lifted himself up and took it between his lips. He went down a little, came back up, then went down a little farther, taking me a fraction of an inch at a time.

About the time he'd taken me impressively deep, he started to strain a bit.

I stroked his hair. "Easy," I whispered. "Takes some...practice to train your..." *What's it called? What is— Jesus, Connor, that thing you do with your tongue...* "Gag reflex."

He eased up and focused on using his lips and tongue. On exploring with them. Fuck, I remembered what it was like to go down for the first time, when every inch of flesh was something

136

new and fascinating, and Connor must've been as fascinated as I'd been. He teased with his tongue, mirroring some of the things I'd done to him before, slid his lips up and down, made sure my entire cock had his full attention. Some guys accidentally got their teeth involved at first, but he didn't, and it was just warm, soft contact on sensitive skin.

And then he added his hand.

Oh my God.

"C-Connor, I'm..." I stared up at the sky, my head spinning so fast I couldn't think straight. "I'm gonna..." My eyes rolled back, and I had just enough presence of mind left to force myself not to thrust into his mouth. I held as still as I could, my entire body shaking and *wanting* to fuck his mouth while he licked and sucked me right to the edge.

"Gonna...gonna come."

And that was it. I couldn't hold back.

With the last scrap of self-control I possessed, I stayed still, resisting the urge to fuck his mouth as I came. It didn't help that he kept at it, stroking me right through a powerful orgasm that damn near made me black out.

He stopped, and I sank back down onto the towel. "Holy fuck."

Connor pushed himself up. He wiped an unsteady hand across his lip.

"You okay?" I panted. "I didn't choke you or—"

He silenced me with a kiss. His tongue was salty, and his kiss was aggressive and demanding, and, Jesus, there was nothing this man's lips did that didn't turn me into a whimpering mess.

Panting, he met my eyes. "I didn't think that would turn me on as much as it did."

I grinned. "Surprise!"

"Turns you on too?"

"Very much so. In fact..." I rolled him onto his back. "I want to return the favor."

"Oh, holy—oh my God!" His whole body bucked up off the towel as I swept my tongue along the length of his cock. "Jesus, Aiden..."

I went down on him with every bit as much enthusiasm as he'd gone down on me, making sure he felt just how much he'd driven me insane. I teased him, stroked him, fluttered my tongue here and swirled it there, getting drunk off his moans and tremors.

"D-don't stop." He dragged a shaking hand through my hair. I tightened my grasp on his dick, and he grabbed on to what he could of my short hair, gripping it tight enough to pull, and the sting in my scalp just drove me on. I took him deeper in my mouth, squeezed him harder with my hand, heart pounding and head spinning from the delirious sounds he made.

"Oh my God, Aiden," he slurred. "Holy fuck..."

Whimpering softly, he thrust into my mouth the way I'd tried so hard not to thrust into his, and I loved it, loved the forcefulness and the shattered control, and I groaned with pleasure as I caught myself imagining him fucking my ass with all this abandon and need.

And right then, he lost it completely and came.

Chapter Fourteen
Connor

It took a few seconds for my vision to clear. Even after Aiden stopped, after I sensed him lying down beside me and draping his arm over me, I still couldn't quite see straight. Or think straight.

"You all right?" he asked, his tone playful.

"Uh-huh." I blinked a few times, the rocky outcropping still spinning and blurring above me. "Just...give me a sec."

Aiden kissed my cheek. "Take all the time you need."

As my heart slowed down and I settled back to earth, I turned toward him and drew him down to kiss me. Tasting my own semen had always seemed like something that would turn me off, but all it did was remind me of everything Aiden had just done. As if I could forget.

As he lifted his head, sweeping his tongue across his lips, I said, "Where the hell did you learn to do that? With your mouth, I mean?"

"Practice." He winked. "Lots of practice."

"Damn. I should've known the Internet wasn't a good place to learn this stuff."

Aiden threw his head back and laughed. "Oh my God, no. The Internet is so full of bullshit."

"So I found." I shifted onto my side. "Can't say I didn't try, though."

He kissed my forehead. "Well, whatever you found must've worked, or you're a natural, because I'm not complaining at all about your skills."

"Is there even such a thing as a bad blowjob?"

"Yes." Aiden grimaced. "Believe me, there is."

"Do I want to know?"

He shook his head rapidly.

"Point taken." I looked around at our surroundings, from the rocks above us to the gleaming white sand and bright-blue tide lapping at the beach. "You know, I don't think we'll ever be able to go to a beach without fooling around on it."

"You say that like it's a bad thing."

"Could be a problem on a crowded beach."

"Crowded beaches suck anyway. I like them more secluded. Where I can do"—he ran his fingers over my stomach, grinning when I gasped—"anything I want."

My abs quivered under his fingertips. "Which would be...what?"

Aiden leaned in and kissed me lightly. "Honestly? I want to do everything with you." His fingers drifted up the side of my neck to my cheek. "But only as much as you're ready for."

"Like...fucking?"

I thought he might've shivered. He lowered his head and kissed the side of my neck, and as he worked his way up from my collarbone to my jaw, he murmured, "If you're ready for it, absolutely."

Oh, I was. I'd been ready for a long time. And with Aiden? Absolutely.

Except...

"When it comes to, uh, anal"—God, I felt like an idiot, with my face heating up like this—"do you prefer being, um..."

Aiden raised his head. "Top or bottom?"

I nodded.

He half shrugged. "I usually end up as the bottom in my relationships, but I like it either way." He inclined his head a little. "Do you want to try both?"

"I do, but would you think less of me if I said it scared me?" I cringed at my own question. Could I have sounded a bit more like a clueless kid?

But Aiden shook his head. "No. Not at all. It scared the hell out of me too."

I gulped. "And when you finally got there, was it... I mean, did..."

"Was I justified in being scared?"

"Yeah. That."

"It..." My gut clenched as he broke eye contact. Then he looked at me again. "I'll be perfectly honest. It *can* be painful and miserable. It was for me." He tenderly touched my face. "But if we go there, I will make absolutely sure that it's not that way for you. I promise."

I shivered. "How do you"—heat rushed into my cheeks— "how do you make sure it *isn't*?"

"Lube. Taking it slow. Starting out with something that isn't quite as thick." He held up his hand and wiggled his fingers.

I couldn't help laughing. "So you're okay with, uh, taking it slow? Baby steps?"

"Okay with it?" His eyes widened. "Jesus, yes. I want you to enjoy it." He caressed my face and held my gaze. "I'll take as much time and use as much lube as it takes to make sure you do."

"Thank you" was all I could think to say. "So, your first time. Was it..."

Aiden shifted a little, and I thought he shuddered. "I was with someone who didn't know what he was doing, and to be honest, I don't think he would've cared enough to do it right if he did know how."

I winced. "Really?"

He nodded. "I mean, he used plenty of lube, but I think that was more for his comfort than mine. We went straight from fooling around to him fucking me, and it..." This time, he definitely shuddered. "I was sore for days afterward."

"Jesus."

"Yeah." He took my hands in his. "I promise you that won't happen. And that's assuming I'm on top. You might find you like topping better."

"Guess I'll have to try both and find out?"

"If you want to, I'm happy to switch."

"You prefer one over the other?"

He half shrugged. "Well, like I said, I somehow usually end up being on the bottom, but I definitely like it both ways."

"How do you 'somehow' end up on the bottom?"

Aiden chuckled. "I guess I have a thing for guys who happen to be tops."

Laughing, I raised an eyebrow. "So does that mean I'm probably going to be a top?"

"Not necessarily." He winked. "But if you are, you won't hear me complaining."

I slid a little closer to him, running my hand down his side. "Now I'm curious."

"Yeah?" He kissed me lightly. "So am I."

"And I want you to."

Yorkville 416-393-7660

Toronto Public Library

User ID: 2 ********* 2770

Date Format: DD/MM/YYYY

Number of Items: 3

Item ID:37131190267039
 Title:Hiatus
 Date due:10/12/2018

Item ID:37131205388044
 Title:ADULT FICTION
 Date due:10/12/2018

Item ID:37131179766910
 Title:ADULT FICTION
 Date due:10/12/2018

Telephone Renewal# 416-395-5505
www.torontopubliclibrary.ca
 Monday, November 19, 2018 1:05 PM

"I will." Aiden kissed me again, longer this time. "Not tonight, but I will."

"Tease." I looked him in the eyes. "I mean it, by the way. I really do want to."

"Then we will." His kiss was soft and gentle. "Soon."

"Promise?"

"Promise."

That weekend, I fed my folks a bullshit excuse about needing to study for a big exam that had actually happened last week—ugh, I felt like I was still in high school—and slipped out with Aiden.

"So, want to check out another castle today?" I asked as I buckled my seat belt. "Maybe Nakagusuku?"

"Maybe next time." Our eyes met, and he gave me this little grin that made my knees shake. "I've got someplace else in mind today."

I gulped. "Oh. Okay. Where?"

He shifted into Drive. "You'll see when we get there. You've got a few hours, right?"

"I've got all day." I eyed him playfully. "What'd you have planned?"

Aiden's sunglasses obscured his eyes, but I could sense the mischievous look he was giving me. "You'll see."

We lost ourselves in conversation, as we always did, but that undercurrent of curiosity on my part and knowing playfulness on his was there the whole time. Every time he made a turn, I thought I might have an a-*ha*!-I-know-where-we're-going! moment, but I didn't. The farther we went out into the middle of nowhere, out behind a few tiny farming villages and sugarcane fields that were backed up almost to the coast, the less I could guess where we were.

He drove us down a smooth but barely there dirt road, and stopped when it dead-ended. From here, I could see an enormous beach—we were on the Pacific side—without a single person in sight.

As he killed the engine, Aiden said, "Here we are."

I looked around. Another beach out in the middle of nowhere. Oh God...

Aiden leaned across the console, turned my head gently with a finger on my chin and kissed me. "The other day, you said you were ready. To go further."

I gulped. "I did, yeah."

"Do you still want to?"

Yes. Yes, please. Oh God. Wait. No. I'm... Yes.

I just nodded.

Aiden's lips skated up the front of my throat. "Today?"

Oh. My God.

"Yes." *No. Wait. Fuck.* "Yeah. I do."

He pulled back and looked in my eyes. "You don't have to. Nothing's set in stone, and we can always turn back."

I shook my head. "No. I do want to. Just...go slow."

Aiden's smile made me shiver just like it always did. "Relax. We're not even out of the car yet."

I laughed. "True."

"I promise, though, we'll go slow." He kissed my forehead. "We've got all the time in the world, and there's no one else here."

I gestured at the sun, which was still high in the sky. "Assuming we don't burn, right?"

He laughed. "Oh ye of little faith." He reached back and tapped the backpack. "I thought of everything. Including sunscreen."

"Sunscreen?" I chuckled. "You did think of everything."

"Of course I did. Let's go."

We got out of the car and took his backpack and a large, folded blanket from the backseat. A more or less clear path wound through the undergrowth, and we took it slow through there, scanning either side for any signs of Habu in the weeds. It would be just my luck that we were about to fuck and one of us would get bitten by a snake and require an airlift.

There weren't any snakes, though, and the path took us out onto the sand. This was one of the white-sand beaches. Well, more like tan or gold, but...light colored. Fucking gorgeous too.

Except there weren't any trees. No rocky outcroppings either.

"Isn't much shade, is there?" I asked.

Aiden shrugged. "The sunscreen's SPF 50. We'll be fine." We walked a little ways, and then he dropped the backpack at his feet a few yards from the high-tide line. "This looks like a good spot."

Holy shit. Are we really doing this?

He faced me, and his brow furrowed. "You okay?"

I nodded. "Yeah. Just a bit nervous." I forced a laugh. "Wasn't expecting to do this today."

His expression didn't change as he stepped closer and put a hand on my waist. "It's not too fast, is it?"

"No. Just new." I wrapped my arms around him and kissed him. "But yes, I want to."

"Good."

For the longest time, we just stood there, wrapped up in each other and kissing with the backpack and blanket at our feet. I was hard, I was horny, but I didn't think I'd ever be able to bring myself to rush us through a kiss. Especially not one of these long, gentle kisses with Aiden's fingers in my hair and his cock hardening against mine.

After a while, he met my eyes. I licked my lips. He did the same. Neither of us said a word, but we both knew what we wanted. Silently, we smoothed the blanket out on the sand, making sure not to get any sand on it, and weighed down the corners with rocks. Then Aiden put the backpack on the edge of the blanket within easy reach and toed off his shoes. I did the same, pretending my heart wasn't going a million miles a minute.

He unzipped the backpack and withdrew a white bottle. Gesturing at me, he said, "Take off your shirt. I'll put some of this on you."

I did as I was told and took off my shirt. Aiden did the same. Together, we knelt on the blanket, and Aiden put some sunscreen on his hands.

"C'mere." As he smoothed the sunscreen on my chest, his lips met mine. While he kissed me, his hands slid over every inch of my chest, back and arms, smoothing the lotion onto my skin as if it were massage oil. He kneaded my shoulders and my neck, and, my God, no one had ever made the application of sunscreen sexier than Aiden.

Breathlessly, I whispered, "I should do the same for you."

"Hmm, maybe you should."

I put some sunscreen in my hand, and gestured for him to turn around. I made circles until the sunscreen had disappeared completely, and then did it a few more times just because I wanted to watch my hands glide over his back.

He turned around again, and now our hands were all over each other's bodies, and it had nothing to do with sunscreen. Even as we slipped out of the last of our clothes and made sure our legs were good and protected, I was more interested in kissing him and pressing against him than anything else.

Aiden, it seemed, was on the same wavelength. He laid me down on the blanket, and his kiss was amazing and terrifying and *oh God, are we really doing this?*

As if he could hear my thoughts, he pushed himself up. "If it's too much, we'll stop. You're not committed to anything."

"I want to." I moistened my lips. "I'm just..."

"Nervous?"

I nodded.

"It's okay. Everyone is." He kissed me again, but just quickly and softly. "There's no point of no return. We can stop *any time.*"

I swallowed. "Can we just...slow down?"

"Of course." He eased himself off me and lay on his side. "I'm not in any hurry."

"Okay."

"For what it's worth," he said, running his hand up and down my chest and abs, "my first time was awkward as hell. And yes, it hurt."

I winced.

Aiden stroked my face. "I'm not going to let that happen to you. I want your first time to be amazing." He brushed his lips across mine. "And I promise, I won't hurt you."

He'd assured me of that before, and I knew it from the reading I'd done on the subject, but now that I was facing the very real possibility of being fucked in the very near future, doubts closed in.

"But you said it *can* hurt."

Aiden smirked. "Well, not if you're on top." Then he turned serious and went on. "Even on the bottom, though, I can make sure it doesn't hurt. We've got plenty of lube and plenty of time." He leaned in and kissed me gently. "I'm not going to hurt you, Connor. I promise. That's the last thing I want to do."

"I know," I said and wrapped my arms around him. "I trust you."

"Good. Speaking of..." He leaned away and pulled a few gold-foil packets from his backpack. "I brought condoms, but if you want to go without, I'm clean. Got tested for everything a few months ago and haven't touched anyone since before that."

I glanced at the condoms in his hand. "Do they make that much of a difference? I've heard you can't feel much."

Aiden shrugged. "They feel pretty different, but I'll take that over taking a risk with someone."

"That makes sense." I arched my eyebrow. "But you said you've been tested."

He nodded. "The military tests us for everything under the sun all the time, especially when they're doing overseas screenings."

"And I've never been with anyone."

"So we're probably both pretty safe." He set the condoms close by, where they'd be within easy reach. "But you're calling the shots. Anything you want. Top or bottom. Condoms or bareback. Anything." He pressed his lips to mine and let them linger there for a moment. "And we don't have to fuck if you don't want to."

"I want to."

"Me too." He slid his arm around me as he came down to kiss me again. "However you want it."

I wrapped my arms around him. As we kissed, our bodies moved like they had minds of their own, his hips rubbing against mine and mine moving just right to complement him. It was like our bodies wanted us to be fucking, and so they did the best they could to get as close as possible to actually doing it while our minds still kept us from dropping the hammer. The more we touched like this—dicks rubbing together, hands all over hot, lotion-coated skin—the more my nervousness gave way to need. I wanted to know what it was like to move inside him, or to feel him moving inside me, and all I had to do was say the word.

And when I did say the word...top or bottom?

Holding him tighter, kissing him harder, I saw myself fucking him, and I saw him fucking me, and I didn't know which way to go.

"I'm not going to hurt you, Connor," I heard him say, *"I promise. That's the last thing I want to do."* I couldn't imagine any man on the planet being so gentle and attentive, or being so determined not to let me feel any pain. Maybe all guys were like that, maybe most of them were, but all I knew for sure was that this one was.

As our lips separated, I whispered, "I want you on top."

Aiden shivered. "Are you sure?"

I nodded. "Yes. I want you to—" I paused, heat rushing into my cheeks. "I want you to fuck me. Bareback."

He exhaled hard, shivering in spite of the tropical sun blazing over our heads. "God, you have no idea how bad I want you."

Drawing him in, I said, "Likewise."

"You can still say stop." He dropped a brief kiss on my lips. "Any time."

I nodded.

Then Aiden lifted himself off me and lay back on the blanket. Gesturing at himself, he said, "Get on top."

"But I—"

"Trust me." The gleam in his eyes made my mouth water.

And I did trust him, so I moved on top, straddling him, and as he nudged my hips up, I realized what he had in mind.

"This way you're in total control." Aiden slid his hands up my abs to my chest. "You decide how fast we go, how deep, everything." As his thumb circled my nipple, he added, "And you can stop any time."

"I know."

"There's lube in the bag." He gestured at his backpack. "Could you grab it?"

I leaned away and riffled around in the bag, quickly finding the small bottle. The clear liquid was almost blinding under the bright sun, and Aiden squinted as I handed it to him.

"Guess they don't make this stuff in 'low glare', do they?"

I laughed, but the sound gave away my nerves, especially as I watched him pop the cap on the bottle.

"Relax. This won't hurt." He handed the bottle back to me, and while I capped it and set it aside, Aiden put a little bit of lube on his fingers. Then he slipped his hand between us, and I shivered as his fingers drifted past my balls and toward my ass

"Breathe," he whispered.

Closing my eyes, I slowly exhaled, and as I did, his fingertip circled my entrance gently, not pressing in, just being there and teasing. It was an odd sensation, being touched there, but it wasn't unpleasant.

Then there was some light pressure.

And then the tip of his finger slid in.

I gasped, tensing a little. "Fuck..."

"Relax." Aiden withdrew his finger but didn't pull it away completely. "Am I hurting you?"

"No. Doesn't hurt." I shook my head. "Just...different."

His other hand ran up and down my thigh, his touch gentle and reassuring. "Just keep breathing and relax. If it hurts, we can stop."

I just nodded.

He kept his hand on my thigh, and with the other, pressed against me again. The fingertip slipped in, out, in again. Then farther in, sliding a little deeper with each stroke as my body got used to the gentle invasion. Somewhere in the back of my mind, I was reeling from the fact that he was fucking me, even if it was only with a finger, but I couldn't hold on to that thought. I couldn't hold on to anything except how good this felt.

With his hips and his free hand, Aiden encouraged me to move, and before I knew it, my body was moving on its own, just like we both had while we'd been pressed together earlier. I wanted to feel his finger moving in and out, so I moved up and down, and, holy fuck, it felt good.

And then he added a second finger. The slight burning, stretching sensation was...addictive. Not uncomfortable, like I thought it would be. It distantly registered as vague pain, but it felt good.

I rode his hand faster. He curled his fingers, then pushed them apart a little, enough to intensify that stretching feeling, and I lost my breath.

"Like that?" He sounded as winded as I was.

I nodded. "Yeah."

"Doesn't hurt?"

"Doesn't hurt." I moistened my lips and forced my eyes open. Oh my God, he was gorgeous, looking up at me like this, pupils blown and lids heavy. And shifting my gaze lower, I saw his thick, hard cock, between us but completely neglected. Meeting his eyes again, I whispered, "I want you. I want..." Words. Fuck. Needed to form words.

"If you want me to fuck you," he whispered unsteadily, "just say the word."

"Yes."

His fingers moved a little faster inside me. "You sure?"

I nodded. "Yes. I'm sure. Aiden, please..."

As he withdrew his hand, I bit my lip. There were still some nerves, some worries, but the only thing at the forefront of my mind was how badly I wanted his dick in me. At this point, I didn't even care if it *did* hurt.

Aiden nudged me up a little, and as he reached for the lube, the world spun around me. The sun was beating on my back, the sand shifting a little under my knees, but the only thing I really felt was the absence of him. As he stroked the lube onto his cock, I was damn near whimpering with not just anticipation but desperation. I'd had a little taste, I'd taken his fingers, but now that seemed as close to the real thing as when we'd been frotting earlier. It just wasn't enough.

I needed more.

I needed his cock.

The click of the lube bottle made me shiver. As he tossed it aside, the liquid glinted in the sun, but I noticed it for only a split second, because then Aiden was stroking more lube onto himself, and when our eyes met, I was sure I was going to come just thinking about taking the next step.

"You ready for—"

"*Yes.*"

He grinned. "You have any idea how hot you are when you're this turned on?"

I licked my lips. "Goddammit, Aiden..."

His grin broadened. I was sure he was going to tease me even more and drive me absolutely insane, but then, with a hand on my hip, he guided me up a bit more. Then he eased me down, and I gasped when his cock pressed against me.

"Take it slow," he said. "There's no rush."

Easy for you to say.

Still, I took the advice to heart. It was tempting to come down fast and take as much of him as possible, but I did as he told me.

"Bear down a little," he whispered.

I did, and...

God.

Oh my God.

The head of his cock slipped in. The stretching burned a little more than it had with his fingers, but it still wasn't painful. Not even uncomfortable, really. It was fucking addictive.

"Lift up a little," he said.

I did, and then, as he gently pressed on my hip, came down again. This time I took him deeper. Jesus, he felt incredible. A hundred people could've suddenly materialized on the beach, and I wouldn't have cared.

Aiden ran his hand up my side. "How does...how does that feel?"

"Good." Understatement. But I couldn't articulate anything beyond that, couldn't even think of anything beyond it. A little at a time, I inched lower, taking more of him.

"Fuck, Connor..." He closed his eyes and exhaled, fingers twitching on my hips. "Fuck, you feel..." He trailed off in a moan.

"This is amazing," I slurred.

"Mm-hmm." He looked up at me, his expression somewhere between blissed out and delirious. "I knew it would be. Knew you would be."

I leaned forward and kissed him. I rested on my forearms, the sand shifting beneath the blanket as I kept rocking back and forth, riding his cock while we lazily explored each other's mouths. He wrapped his arms around me, his skin almost as hot against mine as the sun beating down on my back.

A shiver ran through me, and I broke the kiss with a gasp. Then I let my head fall beside his, my body moving like it knew what it was doing, even while I didn't, and I struggled to catch my breath. God, even the scent of him—sweat, coconut sunscreen—turned me on.

"Sit up," he murmured in my ear. "Lean back a bit."

I sat up. Aiden did too. He wrapped his arms around me again, and he raised his chin to kiss me, and then he was in motion. No, that wasn't right. I was. Rising and falling, riding him slowly because this position wouldn't allow anything else. We kissed, and I moved, and between the sun and the sand and the skin and the sex, I was overwhelmed. Completely lost in him and in the orgasm that was building as Aiden's cock slid easily in and out of me.

A low, throaty groan vibrated against my lips. After a moment, I realized the groan had been mine. I'd had a million orgasms in my life, but the way this one was building was mind-blowing. The tension spread all through my body, my toes curling on top of the blanket and my back arching just right to press me against Aiden, and every time one of us moved with my cock between us, we created the most incredible friction.

"Come for me," he murmured, and as I threw my head back, he kissed my neck. "I know you're close, Connor, I can feel it."

"F-fuck…" I dug my nails into his back, shivering when he pulled in a hiss of breath beside my throat. "God, Aiden, I'm so…so…"

"Let go," he pleaded. "I want to come, but not until—"

That was it.

I was gone.

A tremor shot through me, and then Aiden groaned and shuddered, and I thought one of us released something like a sob as we gave in. I tried to keep riding him, but I had zero control over anything now. There was nothing I could do but hold on to him and come, and he managed to thrust up into me a few more times before he shuddered again.

As my orgasm tapered, I sighed. My spine turned to liquid, so I slumped against him. He held me tight, and slowly we sank back onto the blanket. His stomach and mine were both wet with semen, and his cock was still inside me, and we were both so out of breath we couldn't even kiss, so we just lay there, panting and shaking.

And he'd been right. It didn't hurt.

And it was absolutely amazing.

Chapter Fifteen
Aiden

"You okay?" I whispered in Connor's ear.

"Yeah." He lifted himself up on unsteady arms. "You?"

I caressed his face. "I feel great."

"Me too." He came down and kissed me softly, then carefully rose off me. We both gasped as my cock slid free, and Connor collapsed onto the blanket beside me with an exhausted groan.

I'd brought a few extra towels, which we used to clean ourselves up. Then I draped a larger beach towel over our waists—we had sunscreen on, but I wasn't keen on a sunburned dick—and we lay on our sides, facing each other.

Still breathing hard, he grinned at me. "Never thought my first time would be sex on the beach."

I laughed. "Well, I figured it would be...different."

"It was awesome."

"Good."

We held each other close and kissed lazily, savoring the afterglow. The sun was starting to get low in the sky, though, so after a while, we got up, shook the sand out of our clothes and dressed.

I put the blanket, lube and unopened condoms in the backpack, and then looked around to make sure we hadn't forgotten anything. "Looks like we're ready to go."

"Yeah, but we don't have to go quite yet." He put his hands on my waist and kissed me. "And by the way, thank you. Today was... It was awesome."

I ran my fingers through his hair, brushing free a few grits of sand. "It was awesome for me too." I paused. "And I didn't hurt you or anything, did I?"

"No. Not at all." His smile was equal parts shy and excited. "In fact, I'm looking forward to doing it again."

"Me too." I wrapped an arm around his waist. "I get the feeling we won't be seeing much of the island for a while."

Connor laughed. "None of it's going anywhere. And there's a million places I want to take you to snorkel, but after today, I don't think we'd make it past the beach."

"We never make it past the beach anyway."

Connor laughed. "We have a few times."

"Yeah, but now..." I ran a fingertip down the side of his neck to his collar. "I think I'd rather do this than snorkel."

"But the stuff underwater is so cool."

"Mm-hmm." I hooked my finger in his collar and tugged him toward me. "But you turn me on too much to care about that stuff."

"Point taken." He wrapped his arms around me and kissed me. "I definitely want to do this again."

"Me too."

Another kiss, and this one went on. And on. And on. Connor's hands drifted up my back. Mine slid over his hips. He was getting hard again, and so was I.

"If we keep this up," I murmured between kisses, "we're not going to get out of here."

"Well, damn." Connor kissed me again. "Maybe we should take the blanket out again."

"Maybe we should."

Applying sunscreen as a form of foreplay had been hot. I hadn't thought of doing that before, but in the moment, it'd seemed like a pretty damned good idea, and, really, I wasn't going to say no to sliding my hands all over Connor.

In hindsight, though, it occurred to me it might not have been the most practical idea. I winced whenever I moved in my chair and my shirt or my waistband brushed that strip across my lower back that hadn't been adequately covered. Every time the starched collar of my uniform rubbed against the back of my neck, I felt like an utter moron.

We'd put on sunscreen, but, of course, we hadn't exactly made sure it was evenly distributed. We'd been so excited and caught up in Connor's first time, we'd half-assed the sunscreen, and now... Well, I was burned. My right arm was almost completely unscathed. My left had a band of red starting just above my elbow and another up the back toward my shoulder, but my forearm was fine.

Oh well. At least the burn hadn't been too bad—enough for Shane and Gonzales to rib me about being hemmed up for destruction of government property, but not *that* bad. And burn or not, yesterday had been absolutely amazing. So much better than I'd imagined, and those fantasies had been incredible.

Much as I liked being on top, I'd nearly always been the bottom. I'd just always been attracted to natural tops. And I didn't mind. I loved being fucked.

It had been a long time, though, since I'd been on top, and, Christ, I'd almost forgotten how much I loved being inside someone. For that matter, I couldn't remember ever enjoying it as much as I had yesterday. Just thinking about the way Connor and I had fucked made me shiver. It had all been new to him, completely new, and every time his eyes had widened or his breath had hitched, I'd nearly gone crazy myself.

He'd been in no hurry at all. He was turned on—my God, weren't we both?—but maybe because everything was so new to him, he'd been perfectly happy to take our time. Maybe because it was all overwhelming, maybe because he'd wanted to savor every new experience. I didn't know. All I knew was it had been unrushed and amazing.

My phone vibrated and startled the hell out of me.

We need to do that again.

I laughed and answered: *Yes, we do. Soon.*

Definitely soon. You off work at the usual time?

Yes.

See you then. ;)

I grinned like a goddamned idiot. Just a few more hours. Maybe we'd fuck again, maybe we'd just fool around, or, hell, maybe we'd just find a restaurant or a castle or any place in the world and just sit and talk. I didn't care.

And when had any other guy given me this fluttery, giddy feeling? Never. I'd never felt it before. Not even for my deepest crushes or the two guys I'd ever been in love with. I couldn't wait to see him. Couldn't wait to do...whatever we ended up doing tonight. Snorkel, fuck, eat, hike, talk. Didn't matter. Just let me see him again.

Just a few more hours.

And in the meantime...

Right. Work.

I took a long drink from my ice-cold water bottle. This uniform would not hide a thing if I got carried away with my fantasies, so I needed to calm the fuck down before someone came into my office. Or before I had to go into anyone else's office.

Especially since it was time for my usual rounds to all the officers who needed to sign on dotted lines.

Colonel Patterson. Captain Warren.

And of course, General Bradshaw.

I cringed at the sight of his name on some of the papers. Looking him in the eye had been tough enough since he'd caught me with Connor. Now that I'd had sex with him?

Shaking my head, I gathered up the papers and started my rounds. I didn't know why I was so freaked out. Connor and I had kept things on the down-low, and though Bradshaw never wasted an opportunity to give me a dirty look, as far as I could tell, he believed his son and I were obediently staying apart.

But just for the sake of my sanity, I went to his office first to get that little visit out of the way. Stomach roiling, I knocked on his door.

"It's open."

I stepped into the room and handed over his share of the stack of folders under my arm. Then, as I always did, I stood there like an idiot in front of his desk, waiting for him to peruse everything I'd given him. This was part of my routine, one of the things I hated with any of the officers I dealt with on a daily basis, but with Bradshaw it drove me insane. Though I'd finally accepted that he didn't suspect anything between Connor and me, just being in the same room with him made me nervous.

Bradshaw gave me an icy glare as he handed me the folders. He didn't let go of the folders. For a few unsettling seconds, we both held on to the folders like we were engaged in a paper tug-of-war. Then he released the folders.

"Dismissed, Ensign."

"Thank you, sir." Almost in the clear. I turned to go, trying not to look like I was in too big a hurry. Sprinting for his door and tumbling out into the hall would be less than conspicuous.

As I reached for the doorknob, Bradshaw spoke again.

"That's quite a sunburn, Ensign."

I glanced down at my arm. Sure enough, my sleeve had pulled up enough to reveal the red skin above my elbow. Turning around, I self-consciously tugged it back down, though it didn't do a damned bit of good. "It's, uh, just from resting my arm against the window while I was driving."

His eyebrow flicked upward. "Is that right?"

I nodded.

"I see." He picked up his pen and flipped open another folder. "Might I recommend some sunscreen next time?"

"Noted, sir."

"Dismissed, Ensign."

Thank God.

I got the hell out of his office. Finally in the clear and safely out the door, I still had to deal with the captain and the colonel, but at least—

My stomach suddenly plummeted to my feet, and I froze midstep.

"It's, uh, just from resting my arm against the window while I was driving."

"Is that right?"

This was Japan. Cars were right-hand drive. If my excuse had been true, it would've been my right arm that was burned, not my left.

Oh. Fuck.

A mild sunburn wasn't a career-threatening offense, but feeding a bald-faced lie to the man who was watching me like a hawk over an order not to see his son? Bad idea. Real bad idea.

The rest of my rounds could wait. I went back to my office and sank into my chair, elbows on my desk and fingers pressing into my temples. I hoped and hoped and fucking hoped that the general hadn't looked closely enough to realize which arm was burned and which arm would've been if my story had checked out.

I still didn't regret yesterday. General Bradshaw could send me to the ends of the earth to keep me away from his son, but he couldn't take yesterday away.

But something told me we weren't going to keep this below his radar for long.

Chapter Sixteen
Connor

The only reason I managed to finish any of my homework was the weeks of practice I'd had recently. Every single day had been an exercise in studying and writing papers while counting down the minutes until Aiden was off work, and I'd gotten pretty damned good at it. Just as well we'd waited this long to finally have sex—I'd have failed out of every class by now if we'd jumped right in.

Giddy and distracted, I stared out my bedroom window at the ocean below. I still couldn't believe yesterday had happened. In all the fantasies I'd had about finally sleeping with someone, I hadn't even come close to the reality. Sex on the beach? With someone who was so careful to make sure he didn't hurt me? It couldn't have been any more perfect than it was.

I'd been scared to death that sex would hurt. And, yes, I was a little tender today, but it wasn't even all that uncomfortable—definitely less so than the sunburns or those grains of sand I couldn't quite chase out of my shoe. It was just a reminder whenever I moved that yesterday had really happened.

I felt great today. I couldn't wait to do it again.

I looked down at the open book in front of me. Studying. Right. I was supposed to be doing that.

I reached for the glass I kept on my desk, but it was empty. Good enough excuse as any to get up and stretch for a few minutes, so I stood, stretched and then took the glass downstairs to refill it.

The door to the garage opened. I could tell by the sharp footsteps that it was my father, and out of habit, I tensed.

He doesn't know, I reminded myself. *Fucking chill.*

Dad pulled a pitcher of iced tea out of the fridge. "Is your stepmother home?"

"I think she went to the commissary with Rika."

"Oh, right." As he poured himself a glass of tea, he said, "Ensign Lange had an interesting sunburn when he came to work this morning."

My blood turned cold. His eyes shifted, and the burn on my forearm prickled like he was looking right through my toasted skin.

He set the iced-tea pitcher aside and eyed me over the kitchen island. "Don't lie to me, Connor. Were you with Ensign Lange yesterday?"

Blood pounded in my ears. He had me backed into a corner, and he knew it. If the burns hadn't given us away, my hesitation did.

I set my jaw and narrowed my eyes. "Yes. I was with Aiden yesterday."

"Where were you?"

Having hot sex on top of hot sand.

I casually reached for the pitcher of iced tea. "Does it matter? You don't want us to see each other. We saw each other." I shrugged and started pouring my drink. "What else is there to discuss?"

He didn't say anything, but I could feel him glaring at me. I concentrated on filling my glass and putting the pitcher away. It wasn't a passive-aggressive thing. I just desperately needed to do *something* besides withering under that stare that probably had the same effect on guys who were several pay grades above Aiden.

"Connor." Dad's voice was quiet, but I didn't let my guard down.

I faced him, holding on to that ice-cold glass for dear life. I wanted to believe that thousand-yard stare didn't work on me, but who was I kidding?

He took a drink and set his own glass down. "Listen, son. You know damn well I'm not in this to keep you from getting out and meeting people. I've never forbidden you from dating." He inclined his head, eyeing me. "But not men under my command."

"Dad, we've been over this. Almost every American on this island *is* under your command."

"Then you'll have to wait until you're off the island," he snapped, but quickly softened. "Connor, you don't understand how complicated this can get with his career and with mine."

"Oh, so now it can affect yours?" I folded my arms across my chest. "Fucking really?"

"We've discussed this before. It's a conflict of interest. Borderline fraternization." He sighed, and his voice softened a little more. "Ensign Lange and I work together, and I work directly with his commanding officer. If he gets a promotion or a commendation, or even so much as a 'Nice job, Ensign', how can he or I prove it had nothing to do with his relationship with you?"

I dropped my arms. Painful as it was, I couldn't argue. Military politics were a reality I'd been all too aware of since I was a kid, and whether my dad was a dick about it or not didn't change the fact that fraternization and all that bullshit really could fuck his career. And Aiden's. Goddammit.

"I've never said this was easy for you," Dad said, his tone a little softer now, "but you and I both know it was the lesser of two evils. It was either this or living with your mother, and—"

"Stop." I put up a hand. "Don't make this about Mom."

He fell silent.

"Or if you do," I said, every word carved in ice, "let's talk about how you've used what she did to keep me under your thumb."

"What? I have—"

"Cut the crap, Dad."

His eyes widened.

I continued. "Every time I step out of line, you remind me I have other options. Why don't you just out and say it? If I don't follow your orders to the goddamned letter, you'll send me back to either fend for myself or live with her."

My father glared at me. "I'm not keeping you under my thumb, Connor. This isn't an easy situation for any of us. The fact is, if you date someone under my command, it could fuck his career *and* mine."

"So what am I supposed to do?" I threw up my hands. "Just hold off on dating until I graduate?"

He exhaled. "It's two years, Connor. I know it's not easy, but it's—"

"Not easy? Dad, I'm twenty years old, and Aiden's the first guy I've ever dated! You were married when you were a year older than me."

Dad lifted an eyebrow. "And divorced a few years later."

"Beside the point. You're not even giving me the chance to test the water and find someone."

He sighed. "Look, I'm sorry you're unhappy. Things would be different if we lived in the States, but we don't. I can't change the fact that most of the men your age on this island are military. But it's only two more years."

"Only." I shook my head. "That's a long fucking time to be alone. And for God's sake, what if I really like Aiden?" I hated the way my voice wavered, but couldn't keep it steady. "I don't want to wait two years to be able to date anyone. Aiden's the one I want to see."

Dad held my gaze for a long moment. Then he shook his head. "I'm sorry, son. This one's out of my hands."

Well. What else was there to say?

We broke eye contact. After a moment of awkward silence, Dad left the room, and I stared into the iced tea that I'd barely touched.

This was horseshit, but what could I say? As long as Aiden worked with my father, I couldn't justify putting both of their careers on the line. The day Aiden stopped working for him would either be the day Dad retired or the day Aiden transferred off the island.

I'd heard for years that most Americans eventually got burned out living on this island, because of the isolation. Being on a tiny rock in the middle of the ocean, five thousand miles away from the continental US, could do strange things to people's heads. I'd never understood it. Maybe because being here meant being far, far away from my mother, and because I loved this place.

But suddenly I understood that isolated feeling. I could walk out the door right now, get in the car and drive in any number of directions, but I could only go so far. Any place I went would still be within fifty miles of this house. And my dad. And Aiden.

There was nowhere I could go on this island and get away.

And as long as I couldn't get away from my father, I couldn't be with Aiden.

What the fuck did I do now?

Chapter Seventeen
Aiden

My sunburn faded, turning from red to a tan that I'd never be able to completely even out. I didn't know how Connor's had healed, though, because I hadn't seen him. Ever since that day at the beach, our texts had been brief and sporadic. Any suggestion of getting together was met with a noncommittal response.

We stayed in contact, though, which was promising. Sort of. The more we texted back and forth without seeing each other, the more I wondered if he was just humoring me. He was new to this whole relationship thing, never mind the physical aspect, so maybe he just didn't know how to call it off. At least a dozen times, I psyched myself up to call him and end it, but I never could go through with it. I'd never been able to break up with someone via text or phone. It had to be in person or it felt like a cop-out.

Only problem was getting him to commit to meeting up. And now it had been a good three weeks since I'd seen him. If we did get together, it was anyone's guess if I'd call it off the instant we saw each other, or throw myself at him because, goddammit, I missed him.

Break it off? Yeah, right.

Three weeks since I'd seen him, and I couldn't stop thinking about him. Or why he didn't want to see me. Crap. Had I fucked up? Had that day been too much, too fast? He'd wanted it, but...had he? Did he regret it? Oh God, had I hurt him? Just thinking about it made me break out in a cold sweat.

I'd been slow and careful, giving him as much control as I could, but had that been enough? Was he ashamed? Embarrassed? Did I do something wrong?

I stared at my phone. This wasn't a conversation we could have via text. And I wasn't even sure if we should have it over the phone. In person. It had to be in person.

Holding my breath and dreading the answer, I wrote out a text: *I'd really like to see you.*

After hesitating for one minute, then another, I finally made myself send it.

And then I waited. And waited.

Fuck.

That wasn't good.

I gnawed my lip and drummed my fingers on the desk. Crap. This was the moment of truth, wasn't it? He was probably sitting there, staring at my message and trying to formulate a tactful response.

Almost fifteen minutes later, a message finally came through: *I want to see you too.*

I held my phone to my chest and sighed, giving myself a moment of melodramatic relief, because God *damn*, he'd kept me hanging.

With my heart in my throat, I wrote back: *When?*

And once again, the silence dragged on. And on. And on.

I distracted myself with getting caught up on e-mails, surfing the Web and, finally, playing a mind-numbing video game.

Beside my computer, my phone vibrated. I damn near fell out of my chair when I lunged for it, but I recovered and managed not to drop the thing on the floor. When I looked at the caller ID, my stomach flipped at the sight of Connor's name.

His message, though, almost knocked me out of my chair all over again:

Can you get away for the weekend?

That was a switch.

Swallowing hard, I wrote back: *Yeah, I can.*

Cool. Dad will be in Sasebo until Monday.

Maybe that was what this was about. He and his father must've had it out, and he'd wisely been laying low.

Then a longer message came through.

If you can reserve a place at the Okuma resort, I'll pay for half. For Saturday night? Put it under your name. I'll meet you there.

"Thank God."

I'll make the reservation now. See you this weekend.

Less than a minute later, he replied: *I'll see you then.*

Connor beat me to the resort, and I'd never been so happy to see his car.

He was parked beside the main office of the resort, and as I pulled into the lot, he came out of the little shop next to the office.

I got out of the car, and his eyes lit up.

"You made it," he said, striding toward me.

"Did you think I wouldn't?"

He didn't answer. He just threw his arms around me. For a split second, I was aware of the fact that we were in public, but he kissed me so hard he almost knocked me off my feet, and I didn't care anymore. We were in public. At an American resort. With Americans around.

And fuck it. Just...fuck it.

I ran my fingers through his hair and returned his kiss, not giving a damn who saw or who cared. Even if I couldn't hide this growing hard-on, I just didn't care.

"I'm so glad you came," he said.

"Me too." I dipped my head to kiss his neck. "I was afraid you didn't want to see me."

"I've been dying to see you." He shivered and arched his throat against my lips. "After last time, I've..."

"It wasn't too much for you?"

"God, no." He dragged his fingers through my hair. "The last time was amazing. I've been losing my fucking mind ever since then." Connor sighed. "My dad got on my case. He threatened to—"

"It's okay. You don't have to justify yourself." I raised my head and kissed him tenderly. "I just missed you, that's all."

"I missed you too." He licked his lips. "Maybe we should go check into our cabin." With a wink, he added, "It's more private."

"Yes. Yes, it is." I took his hand, and we both subtly—well, as subtly as anyone could—adjusted the fronts of our shorts before we went into the resort office.

On the way out, Connor held up the keys to the golf cart that came with our cabin. He smirked. "A golf cart? Seriously?"

"Yeah. They don't allow cars out there, and it's a bit far to walk."

"At least it'll get us there faster than on foot."

"You haven't ridden in too many golf carts, have you?"

Connor laughed. "No, but it's gotta be better than walking with a hard-on." He winked, and I shivered.

I tossed my overnight bag into the back of the cart and slid in beside him. He put a hand on my leg, and I covered his hand with mine. We exchanged grins, and, goddammit, I was already getting hard again.

I drove the cart as fast as it would go, which wasn't what I'd call fast, but it got us across the resort to our cabin.

The cabin was tiny, tucked up against a bluff on the edge of a private beach that was reserved for guests renting this particular spot. The whole place was ours. Completely ours.

I parked in front of the cabin. "Here we are."

We both got out of the cart. I grabbed my bag, and we hurried up to the front door. Connor unlocked it. As soon as we were inside, I hadn't even let go of my bag before he grabbed me and kissed me.

My bag fell to the floor at our feet. Connor's landed on top of it. Embracing him, I nudged the bags away with my foot so we wouldn't trip over them. Jesus fuck, I'd missed the way he kissed. Our overnight bags were the least of our worries right then—I was lucky my legs stayed under me at all.

"Maybe we should test out that bed," I said.

Connor shivered, pressing his hardening cock against me through our shorts. "Maybe we should." He kissed me again. "I don't know if I mentioned this, but I've missed you like crazy."

"You mentioned it." I ran my fingers through his hair. "But that's okay. I missed you too. So fucking bad."

"I wanted to see you," he said, the words coming quickly. "But my dad, he figured out we'd been together, and—"

"I know." I held him against me and kissed his forehead. "He didn't say anything to me, but I know damn well he knew."

Connor sagged against me. "I feel like such an idiot for—"

"Don't." I cupped his jaw, tilted his head up and kissed him softly. "It's on him, not you."

"I know, but..." He sighed.

"I mean it," I whispered. "Don't. You didn't do anything wrong." I silenced his protest with another kiss and added, "Now let's test out that bed."

Connor laughed and nudged me back a step. "I like that idea."

Still dressed, we tumbled onto the bed together. It was hard and smallish, but it would do just fine. We didn't need much space, and a hard mattress just meant more leverage when I was inside him and wanted to give him more, harder, faster—

"Fuck, I want you." He kissed me, his body shuddering on top of mine, and I was so damned turned on my head was spinning.

"Me too. I haven't been able to stop thinking about you." I brushed my lips across his. "You're all I've been able to concentrate on since we met."

"Me too," he said. "I'm lucky I can study at all."

"Good thing you don't have to study now." I pushed his T-shirt up. "For the next twenty-four hours, it's just you and me."

"Thank God," he growled. He sat up, peeled off his T-shirt and came back down to me. Oh fuck, now my hands were on his hot, bare skin, running all over him and feeling him and dying to have him completely naked. Tugging at his belt, I could barely remember how to maneuver the buckle. God, I really had missed him. I'd been twisting in the wind, physically aching for him, as well as wondering if I'd pushed him too far, but now that he was in my arms again, I realized it had been more than lust and fear keeping him on my mind 24/7.

There was something between us that I'd never felt before. Something that kept drawing me back to him, even when we had to meet in secret for the sake of my career and his peace at home. There was lust—fuck yes, there was plenty of that—but it wasn't just the nearest warm body that had me losing my mind like this. It was Connor and no one else.

And if I didn't get him naked *right now*, I was going to require paramedics.

"I want you to fuck me again," he whispered.

I groaned and pressed against him. "I've been dying to hear you say that."

"And I've been dying to do it."

"Then let's get these clothes off." I kissed him once, brief and hard, and let him up. We stripped down to nothing, and then I got up, leaving the bed just long enough to get the lube from my overnight bag.

As I returned, Connor plucked the lube bottle from my hand. "Let me."

"Already? No foreplay?"

He smirked. "Three weeks of jerking off doesn't count as foreplay?"

"Good point." I joined him on the bed as he poured some lube in his palm, and before I'd even settled beside him, his hand was on me. His fingers were slick, simultaneously cool from the lube and still hot, and my eyes rolled back as he made slow, tight strokes up and down my cock.

"C-careful." I curved a hand around the back of his neck and kissed him. "You'll make me come too soon."

"We've got all night." He twisted his hand slightly, which blurred my vision. "If you come now, I'll just wait till you recover."

"But then— Fuck, Connor." I released a ragged breath as a shudder went up my spine. "Then I'll have to wait to fuck you. And I...cannot wait anymore."

Connor's hand slowed. "I can't either."

"Put some lube on my hand," I said.

"Hmm?"

"Just do it."

He poured some lube on my fingers. Then I kissed him again, and, still kissing, we sank all the way down to the hard mattress.

As I slid my hand up his inner thigh, he parted his legs but growled, "Just fuck me. No fingers."

"I will." I brought my hand up higher, letting my palm drift across his balls, which made him gasp. "But like I told you before, I don't want to hurt you."

Whatever protests he had died when my fingers traced the edge of his crack.

"I want to fuck you so bad I can't see straight," I murmured, pressing my fingertip against him. "But I'm not going to hurt you."

He exhaled, screwing his eyes shut as I pressed a slick finger into him. He was tight but offered almost no resistance, and he moaned as I added a second finger.

"Jesus Christ." He shuddered, arching off the bed as I slowly fucked him with my hand.

"Like that?" I asked.

"Mm-hmm. But I want your— Oh my God!" His eyes flew open as I crooked my fingers inside him. "Holy. *Fuck.*"

"This okay?"

"Uh-huh. Oh my...God..." He sank back onto the bed, lips apart and eyes watering. "What the hell..."

"Male G-spot." I smothered his moan with another kiss. I bent my fingers again, and he grabbed on to my arm, gripping tightly and rocking his hips to encourage my hand to move faster. I was out of breath when I broke the kiss and managed to whisper, "I think you're ready for more."

He just moaned again.

Slowly, I withdrew my fingers. As I sat up, I grabbed the other pillow and handed it to him. "Put this under your hips."

"What? Why?"

"Trust me." I kissed him gently. "Angle's a little more comfortable."

"Fair enough." He put the pillow under himself. I nudged his knee, and he spread his legs wide.

Guiding myself to him, I struggled to keep breathing steadily and evenly, but the anticipation was almost too much. We'd only done this once—well, twice—and I'd been going crazy wanting it again, and now...

Connor moaned softly as I pressed the head of my cock against him. As I carefully breached him, he closed his eyes and gasped.

"This okay?" I asked. "I'm not hurting you, am I?"

"No, it's good. It's...good." He bit his lip and arched as I pushed deeper inside him. "Oh my God, it's good."

"Just tell me if—"

"I will. But you're good. God, that feels amazing..."

"You're damn right it does." I hooked my elbow under his knee and leaned forward. Just as I'd hoped, he gasped and shuddered just the way he had when I'd bent my fingers.

"Fuck!"

I picked up speed. He was right, it felt amazing. He was the only one I'd ever fucked bareback, and the sensation was unbelievable. Slick, hot, tight—thank God I'd jerked off this morning, or there was no way in hell I would've lasted.

I guided his hand to his own cock, and he got the message. The instant he started stroking, he tightened around me, and my breath caught.

"Oh God," he moaned, squirming as I fucked him and he jerked his own dick. "Oh God, I'm gonna..."

"Come, Connor," I panted. "I'm right there too. Gonna...oh shit..."

He released the most spine-tingling, helpless sound I'd ever heard, a cry somewhere between a sob and a moan, and he clenched around me as semen landed on his abs. Then I realized the cry I'd heard wasn't his but mine, and I fucking lost it. I threw my head back, thrust deep inside him and came.

As we both returned to earth, trembling and panting, I pulled out but didn't get up. "You okay?"

He nodded. "God, yeah. That position is... Holy..."

"Thought you'd like it." Leaning down to kiss him, I added, "And all you have to do is just lie back and enjoy it."

"I'll have to return the favor."

"Any time." I dropped another light kiss on his lips. "For now, though, maybe we should grab a shower."

"Good idea."

It was still the middle of the day, the water glittering in the sun outside, but we weren't in any hurry to leave this cabin. After we'd showered together, we climbed back into bed and pulled a sheet over us.

He tenderly touched my cheek. "So is it a safe bet we won't be able to walk tomorrow?"

"If we can walk tomorrow, we did something wrong tonight."

Connor laughed, and he started to say something, but right then his thumb brushed over my eyebrow, and before I could stop myself, I winced.

"Shit, sorry." He jerked his hand back. "Sorry."

"No, it's okay." I grasped his wrist and kissed his fingers. "Just...still keep expecting it to hurt."

"It's healed, though, isn't it?"

I nodded. "Yeah, but it was pretty sore there for a while."

"Oh. Okay."

I could see the unspoken question in his eyes. I never *had* told him the whole story, not even when he'd asked about it.

I turned onto my side, facing him. "So, when we first started out, you asked about the pictures on my Facebook page. The one of the cuts on my face."

Connor nodded.

I inhaled slowly. "You want to hear the story?"

"Only if you're okay telling it."

"I am." I shifted onto my back, and he rested his head on my chest with my arm around his shoulders. Once we'd more or less settled, I said, "So what happened was, the night before we met, I went to this place called Palace Habu."

"I know that club."

I stiffened and barely resisted the urge to protectively pull him closer. "You do?"

Connor nodded. "Only went once or twice. Seemed like kind of a shit-hole."

"You could say that," I muttered. "Anyway, I met a guy. This Marine." Just thinking about Glenn made my skin crawl. "He seemed all right, and he was pretty good-looking, so we had a couple of beers. And we decided to go someplace else. The...

Well, you've been there. You know that alley that goes from Gate Two Street to the club?"

"Yeah."

"There's an area along that alley where you're pretty much invisible from the road. And about the time we got to that part, he grabbed me and..." I forced back the nausea rising in my throat as I gestured at my eyebrow.

"Oh my God," he whispered. "He did that?"

"Yeah." The memory made me want to shudder, but I suppressed it. "I still don't know how he got the best of me. I've rewound it a million times in my head, and there are so many things I should have done to—"

"Hindsight's twenty-twenty." He put a hand on my arm. "Don't keep doing that to yourself. You can't change it."

"I know. Just...bothers me." I sighed. "Years and years of training for just that sort of thing, and..." *And I choked. And I forgot everything I knew. And I got fucking scared.* "I busted him up a bit too, but still."

Connor didn't say anything. He just moved a little closer to me and draped his arm across my stomach.

I went on. "When I went to the emergency room, the cop who came in to take my statement caught on that something wasn't adding up." I laughed dryly, staring up at the ceiling. "Guess I didn't really think it through, and it was a bit too transparent for him. So he finally got me to admit what happened." I shuddered at the memory of how nervous I'd been until Eric had convinced me he was on my side. "After I did, he told me to go up to Hiji Falls, and then post some pictures saying I'd busted myself up on the rocks."

"Wow," Connor whispered. "Did anything ever happen to the guy?"

"I don't know. The cop told me to stay away from the club for a while, and that he'd handle the guy, but beyond that..." I shook my head.

Connor chuckled. "Maybe he kicked his ass."

"I'd have paid to see that. Dude needed a good ass whooping, and the cop looked like he could've taken him." I turned on my side to face him. "I guess, in a way, it's good that the whole thing happened."

"What do you mean?"

Smiling, I touched his cheek. "If I hadn't gone up to Hiji Falls, I never would've met you."

"Wow. Fate works in mysterious ways, doesn't it?"

Fate. I hadn't even thought about that, but lying here with Connor like this, it made sense. Too many things had to have fallen into place for us to meet.

"Yeah," I said, brushing a few strands of hair out of his face. "I guess it does."

He didn't say anything, just lifted his head and kissed me. As the kiss deepened, the embrace did too, and when he nudged me onto my back, I didn't resist. In fact, I slid a hand between us.

"You're insatiable tonight," he panted against my lips.

Covering his hardening cock with my hand, I said, "You're one to talk."

He just moaned, pressing his dick against my palm. "I want as much of you as I can have tonight."

I shivered and squeezed him. "I'm all yours tonight."

Connor pressed his lips to mine again. We made out, and touched each other, and held on to each other, and as desperate as I was to be inside him again, I was in no rush. I loved everything about this. If it took all night for this to progress to having sex, I didn't care, just as long as we didn't stop.

Forget tonight. I'm all yours.

Breaking a long kiss, Connor touched his forehead to mine, and we just held each other for a moment. My heart was racing in a way it never had before, and it wasn't the sex. It was...this. The two of us this close together, simultaneously relieved to be with him after so long and feeling like we'd never been apart at all.

I don't want to be away from you.

I need you, Connor. I want you and I need you.

I took a breath and was about to speak, but caught myself.

Easy, Aiden. Don't go there.

So I just kissed him instead. Connor wrapped his arms around me, and we sank onto the mattress together. We kissed lazily, and I didn't say a word. Not yet.

I felt it. I knew it.

But tonight wasn't the night to tell him I loved him.

Chapter Eighteen
Connor

We left the cabin for a couple of hours, mostly to kick around one of the villages nearby. Aiden picked up a few pieces of local pottery to send home as gifts, and we found a café with the most amazeballs yakisoba on the island. Then we wandered back to the resort, perused their video rentals and the rack of pamphlets about things to do in the area.

None of the DVDs sounded particularly appealing, so we left with a few munchies, got into our golf cart and headed back to the cabin.

As we got out of the golf cart, I looked out at the beach that was ours as long as we rented the cabin. The sun had set, but the light from the cabin's porch illuminated the whole area. It was smallish, maybe a hundred feet across, and had a well-used fire pit above the high-tide line.

Aiden put an arm around me and kissed my cheek. "Maybe we should spend some time out here."

"Watching the ocean and collecting shells, right?"

He snorted. "Sure."

I winked. "By the way, you'll be thrilled to know I haven't been able to look at a beach without thinking about last time. I'd say you've ruined beaches for me forever, but 'ruined' doesn't seem like the right word."

Aiden laughed. "I'd say I'm sorry, but 'sorry' isn't the right word either."

Chuckling, I rolled my eyes.

"And as you can see, we *have* a beach right here." Aiden grinned. "We can sleep in the bed, but..." He let his raised eyebrows finish the thought.

"At night?"

"Why not? This isn't the desert. It doesn't get cold at night."

"Hmm, true. You get the lube; I'll get a blanket."

Though it was dark, the day's heat and humidity lingered. Still, Aiden built a fire in the pit. We didn't need the heat, but the light would be handy.

While he did that, I laid out the blanket and put rocks on the corners to hold it in place. "At least we won't get sunburned this time."

Aiden laughed. "I hadn't even thought of that. Less evidence, right?"

"Yeah. Maybe we won't get busted this time." More serious now, I watched my fingers run along the side of his face. "I just needed to be with you. Away from everything else." I reached up and stroked his hair. "I'm sorry this has gotten so complicated. With my dad and—"

"Don't." He shook his head. "Circumstances are what they are. This weekend is about us making the best of those circumstances."

"So, sneaking away for sex on the beach?"

"Something like that." Aiden kissed me gently. "And speaking of which..." He wrapped his arms around me, and his kiss said the conversation was most definitely over.

We took our time, just making out on top of the blanket and removing one article of clothing at a time. It was too easy to get caught up in kissing, in exploring freshly bared skin, we kept forgetting ourselves and losing ourselves, getting as far as unbuckling a belt or untucking a shirt before we were tangled up in another kiss.

At some point, Aiden tossed his boxers aside, and there was nothing left between us. Just hot flesh and the humid night air, our fingers running through hair and over naked skin as we kissed like we had all night. Because we did have all night. There was no rush tonight. No need to look over our shoulders, no one who might suspect anything. Until tomorrow afternoon, it was just us. We'd even get to wake up together in the morning, something I hadn't even let myself fantasize about until now.

He broke the kiss and started on my neck, his lips and stubble giving me goose bumps.

"I don't know if I've mentioned this," he said, "but I have never been as turned on as I am when I'm with you."

I bit my lip. "Seriously?"

"Mm-hmm." He worked his way up the side of my neck. "I don't know what it is, but you..." He pressed a kiss just beneath my jaw. "I don't even know." His cock brushed mine, and he rubbed over it again, making me gasp. "No idea, but I don't want to stop."

"Definitely don't want to stop."

He found my lips again and kissed me. I hooked a leg around him, pulling him harder against my dick, and he rocked his hips just right to create that addictive friction. He moved like he was fucking me, his cock sliding against mine, instead of in and out of my ass, and the world spun faster and faster as we kissed and ground together.

Finally, I couldn't wait. "Lube." It was all I could say. If I even breathed the words *I need you to fuck me*, I was going to come, I was sure of it.

Aiden reached for the lube, and when he came back with it, he leaned down to kiss my neck again. "I want you on top this time."

I stiffened. "On top?"

"Mm-hmm." He shivered against me and whispered, "I want *you* to fuck *me*."

Holy shit. I did almost come as he said it, but nerves kept me in check. "I, um, I have no idea what I'm doing."

"Yes, you do." His lips skated along the side of my neck. "Just put on some lube, slide in"—he shivered hard—"and do whatever feels good."

I closed my eyes. "Everything feels good."

"Then do everything." He was panting hard now, his fingers digging into my back as his lips continued exploring the side of my throat. "God, Connor, I want you so bad."

I whimpered and pressed my neck against his lips and my cock against him. "Fuck..."

"Trust me," he murmured. "Your body knows what to do. Just...please..."

"Okay." I sat up and grabbed the bottle of lube.

He sat up too. "Might be easier for you if I'm on my hands and knees."

"Mm-hmm." I didn't move. "But to quote someone I just recently had sex with, then I can't kiss you." I kissed him right then, and Aiden moaned softly, shivering against me.

He drew me down with him so I was on top. Then he reached for the bottle of lube and poured some into his hand. As he drew me closer with his other hand, he started stroking my cock. The lube was cool, his hand was warm, and the anticipation was going to drive me out of my fucking head. We made out, and I fucked his slippery fist, and, damn, this was going to be over before it started, but it felt so good.

His hand slowed, and his lips left mine. "C'mere." Aiden lay back, pausing to put a folded towel under his lower ass, and spread his legs for me.

I hesitated. Holding up my hand, I said, "Should I—"

"No. Trust me." He swept his tongue across his lips. "I'll be fine."

I was tempted to tease the hell out of him, to get back at him for doing the same to me, but maybe another night. When I wasn't this excited and nervous.

I positioned myself between his legs, and I could barely breathe as I pushed against him. Panic skittered up my spine— was I doing it wrong? Was I going to hurt him? Was—

And then I was inside him.

Oh. My. *God.*

Just the head of my cock. Not much, but enough to make the entire world turn white. I met some more resistance and vaguely remembered how Aiden had eased himself in, pulling out almost all the way before pushing in again, and I did the same. With each stroke, he took me a little deeper, and I went a little further out of my mind.

"Jesus..."

"You okay?" he asked.

I nodded and blinked my eyes into focus. "You?"

"Ooh yeah." His foot pressed against my hip, encouraging me forward, and I slid even deeper inside him. Then I pulled out and pushed in again, and, holy fuck, this felt even better than I'd imagined. The entire universe concentrated itself into that slick, tight point of contact. For a few slow, careful strokes, nothing else existed.

I lowered my head to kiss him, and Aiden lifted himself up off the blanket to meet me halfway. He cupped my face in both hands, and I didn't even care that there was still some lube on one as he sank back to the blanket, drawing me down with him. And then he wrapped his arms around me, and I was incapable of having a conscious thought, of figuring out a way to move or a rhythm or anything except how good it felt to move inside him, but I didn't need to think. My body took over. My hips moved, and my cock slid in and out of Aiden, my vision blurring with every tight, slick stroke.

Time might've sped up, or slowed down, or gone away altogether. My body was in control, and I was completely and totally lost in Aiden, in moving with him and against him and inside him. And there was no hurry. No one around to catch us, no reason to rush or hide or do anything other than enjoy every slow, deep stroke. I was in no rush to come, and the way he moved with me, he wasn't either. My muscles burned with exertion, but my head was spinning too fast and my cock felt way, way too good to give a damn.

"Faster," Aiden moaned in my ear. "Oh my God, Connor…"

I gritted my teeth and moved faster. My vision blurred, so I squeezed my eyes shut, but even that didn't help.

"Harder." He was begging now, the desperation echoing across my nerve endings. "Please."

"I can't… I'm gonna…"

"Come," he whispered and rocked his hips just right. "Don't stop until you come."

All the tension broke at once. I shuddered hard and forced myself all the way inside him, and my eyes rolled back as his hips kept moving, kept drawing out the most insane orgasm I'd ever had in my life, and I heard myself curse just before everything went completely white, and then black, and then I collapsed on top of him. Panting and shaking, I tried to lift myself up, but he wrapped his arms around me and held me to him.

"I knew you'd feel amazing." He stroked my hair with an unsteady hand. "And you did."

"So did you." I carefully started pulling out. "But you haven't come yet. I—" I gasped as my cock slid all the way out of him. "I want to make you come."

"You won't have to do much," he murmured, fingers twitching on my shoulders. "*Fuck*, you turn me on."

"Ditto." I kissed his neck and started to move down so I could go down on him, but he stopped me.

"No. Stay right there." He nudged me to lift my head, and when I did, he pulled me into a kiss, and he held me there. "Just...your hand. It's all I—oh my fucking God, *yes...*" He arched beneath me as I stroked his rock-hard cock.

"Lube," he murmured. "Use...use some lube."

I grabbed the bottle and poured some on my hand. Then I reached for his cock again, and all it took was one stroke before Aiden released the most blissed-out groan I'd ever heard. "Ooh, that's perfect."

"Like this?"

"Mm-hmm." He kissed me again, and his hips thrust in time with my strokes, forcing his dick through my grip. I pumped his hard, slippery cock as fast as I could. His fingers dug in painfully hard, and he swore through his teeth as his back arched and his body shook, and then hot semen coated my hand, making it even slicker.

He grabbed my wrist, and when I loosened my grasp, he exhaled. "Just so you know," he slurred, "experienced or not, you did *just* fine."

I laughed, and silly as it was, I really was relieved to hear that. "Might be a good idea to practice, though, right?"

Aiden grinned sleepily. "You can practice on me any time you want."

"Careful what you wish for." I winked. "We've got the whole night and a bottle of lube."

"Bring it on," he murmured.

"For now, maybe we should grab another shower."

"We will." He drew his hand up my spine. "In a minute."

Neither of us was very steady on our feet as we got up to clean ourselves off, but between the two of us, we managed. We returned to the bed where we'd spent the better part of the afternoon. With the sheet over us, we lay on our sides, facing each other.

Even after fucking twice and being with him—naked more than not—for the last few hours, I still couldn't believe he was here. More than that, I couldn't believe how much easier it was to breathe now that he was here. I hadn't even realized how much I'd been lost and fumbling for the last three weeks until that moment when he'd pulled into the resort.

There you are, I remembered thinking. *Finally. There you are.*

When it came to relationships, I didn't have the first clue about, well, anything. I'd never had a boyfriend. I'd never had sex before him. I'd never been in love.

But now I did. And I had. And I was.

Running my fingers through his short hair, looking into his eyes because there wasn't anything else I wanted to look at, I realized this couldn't be anything else. I loved him. If this wasn't love, then I didn't know what the fuck was, because this was...this... I couldn't even fit it into my head.

Aiden smoothed my hair. "You okay?"

I nodded, moistening my lips. "Yeah. Just thinking. About...what we're doing."

"Yeah?" His eyebrow arched. "And?"

I shrugged. "Just trying to figure it all out, I guess."

"Good luck."

"What do you mean?"

"I mean I've been trying to do the same thing, but this thing... It's insane." Stroking my hair, he whispered, "I've never had anything like this with anyone else."

"So it's not just me?"

Aiden smiled. When he shook his head, his stubble hissed across the pillowcase. "No, it's not just you." He traced my jaw with the pad of his thumb. "And it's insane, but I don't want to stop."

"Neither do I." I swallowed. "So where do we go from here? We can't just tell my dad to shove it."

Aiden grimaced. "I don't know. I guess we just keep it quiet for now. Until we figure out what to do."

"Easier said than done."

"I know. But..." He brushed the backs of his fingers across my cheek. "It's worth it. Seeing you is... It's just worth it."

My heart fluttered, and I clasped his hand in mine. "You're worth it too. I'm just worried about—"

"So am I, but I don't want to worry about any of that tonight." He lifted himself up and leaned in to kiss me. Sliding an arm around me, he used his body weight to ease me onto my back. "All I know right now is I want to be with you."

"Then let's not worry about anything else tonight."

"We won't."

He was right.

We didn't.

Chapter Nineteen
Aiden

My eyes fluttered open. For a split second, my unfamiliar surroundings disoriented me, but as I woke up fully, I remembered where I was.

Where we were.

Carefully, I rolled over, and there he was. He was on his stomach, the sheet draped across his hips and his arm dangling off the side of the bed. There were a few marks on his back too. Just faint red marks, no deep bruises or anything. I probably had a few myself. We hadn't gotten particularly rough, but it was amazing how strong fingers could get during moments of passion.

I slid closer to him and gently rested my arm over his back.

He stirred a little, murmuring something, and I kissed the back of his shoulder.

"Morning," I said.

He yawned and started to roll over, so I lifted off him to let him move. Then he smiled up at me, his eyes sleepy. "Morning."

"Sleep well?"

"Better than I have in a long time. You?"

"Same." I ran my fingers across the stubble on his jaw. "You want to go find some breakfast?"

"Breakfast sounds awesome, but I'm gonna grab a shower first." He kissed my cheek. "Want to join me?"

"You go ahead. If I join you, we'll never go get any breakfast."

"Good point."

While Connor showered, I lay back on the bed we'd shared, and stared up at the ceiling. My gut slowly twisted itself into a nervous knot. This was easy in the beginning when it was just some sex we needed to keep under the radar, but what if it was more?

Things with Connor were different than they'd been in the beginning. This wasn't just sex. It wasn't just a little fling with the added thrill of tiptoeing behind a general's back.

This was something real. That was the only way I could sum it up. It was real, and it was unavoidable, and that meant sooner or later, one way or another, Bradshaw was going to find out. And then what?

Because it *was* more than it had been in the beginning. It was way more than I'd bargained for.

Question was, did that mean I was in over my head?

The week after Connor and I slipped away to Okuma, Commander Mays and his wife had a barbecue at their house. A lot of people from our office were there, but not the higher-ups. No Captain Warren, no Colonel Patterson, and—praise every god imaginable—no General Bradshaw.

The people in this command had barbecues all the time. I didn't always come to them, but Connor needed to spend the weekend studying since he hadn't cracked the books once last weekend. Besides, it was nice to hang out with my coworkers once in a while without the uniforms and paperwork.

At least all of us weren't all sick of each other—I'd heard plenty of stories about colleagues driving each other up a wall—

though I noticed Commander Morris never came to these things. I never asked if that was his choice, or if Mays, Gonzales and Shane just didn't extend the invitations. If the rumors I'd heard were to be believed—especially about Morris and Shane being almost literally at each other's throats whenever they all went out to the O-Club after work—I guessed the reason for Morris's absence was a lack of an invite. I didn't mind. What little interaction I'd had with that asshole was more than enough.

Everyone grabbed food from the kitchen where Mays's wife and some of their friends were chatting and cooking, and we sat in the lawn chairs outside. Commander Mays balanced his newborn daughter on one arm, rocking her gently as he sipped his beer. I sat in one of the lawn chairs, a beer in the cup holder and a paper plate balanced on my knee. Mays could barbecue ribs like nobody's business, and Noriko made amazing wings, but I barely tasted them this time. I was just too distracted.

Gonzales sipped her beer. "I think Morris is on his way over."

Shane's head snapped up, and I thought he paled. "What?"

"He'd better not be," Mays said, throwing her a pointed look.

She laughed and held up her hand. "Chill, guys. I was just fucking with you."

Shane relaxed.

"Get a grip." Gonzales elbowed Mays. "You know I don't want him here any more than you do."

"I just don't want him and Connelly killing each other here." Mays nodded toward the house. "Noriko will kill *me* if those two bust the furniture or get blood on that new floor."

"I wouldn't bust the furniture or get blood on the floor." Shane rolled his eyes. "Not when there's a perfectly good parking lot outside for me to curb stomp him."

Gonzales choked on her beer, and both commanders burst out laughing.

"You deserved that," Connelly said.

From my chair, I chuckled. "Well played, Commander."

Shane turned to me. "Commander? Pfft. We're off the clock, kid." He clapped my shoulder. "I've told you once, I've told you a hundred times—I'm only a commander with the uniform on. Just call me Shane."

"Okay." Familiarity with superior officers was a strange thing—the Academy had drilled it into our heads pretty hard that we addressed each other by rank and rank alone—but maybe I'd get used to it eventually.

As we all socialized between swallows of beer and bites of chicken wings, my mind kept wandering back to the weekend I'd spent with Connor. I'd been on edge all week, especially at the office. Bradshaw was still gone, thank God, but he'd be back at work on Monday. What the hell was I supposed to do then?

I glanced at Shane. He kept looking down at his phone and smiling. He quickly wrote something, and then turned the phone screen down on his leg. Must've been MA1 Randall on the other end.

He turned his head, and when we made eye contact, he lifted his eyebrows.

My cheeks burned as I dropped my gaze, trying to find something else to hold my interest. Like the fact that I'd finished my wings. That was as good a diversion as any, so I got up and took my plate into the kitchen.

As soon as I stepped into the kitchen, Noriko turned around and held out both hands. "I take it."

"Are you sure? It's—"

She beckoned with her outstretched hand. "I take."

"Oh. Okay." I handed her the plate. "*Arigato.*"

She gave a small bow, which I returned, and as she headed back into the kitchen, I started toward the patio. So much for my diversion.

Right then, Shane appeared in the doorway. "Hey, kid."

I swallowed. "Hey."

He cocked his head. "You okay?"

"I'm..."

He looked at me for a moment, then looked over his shoulder. "Hey, Mays, how we doing on beer?"

Balancing his daughter on his hip, Mays lifted the lid of the cooler with his toe. "Getting a little low on the Orion. Why?" He lowered his foot and let the lid drop. "You want to make a liquor run?"

Shane nodded. "Yeah. I'll take Lange with me."

I blinked. "I—"

"Come on, kid." He pulled his keys out of the pocket of his shorts. "Let's go."

"Sure. Why not?" I followed him out to his car. "You sure you're good to drive?"

He threw me a look. "After one beer?"

"Hey, I didn't make the rules on this island."

"No kidding," he muttered and got in on the driver's side. "Don't worry about it."

As I buckled myself into the passenger seat, he said, "Anyway, I figured you could use a few minutes to talk in private."

"Thanks. Yeah, actually, I could probably use some advice."

"Okay." He started backing out of the parking space. "What's up?"

"Well, uh, I've been dating someone."

He shifted into Drive and started out of the parking lot. "I'd say congrats on finding a decent, available gay man on this island, but I have a feeling there's a 'but' involved here."

I laughed humorlessly. "Yeah. There is."

"Okay...?"

I stared out the windshield. "I'm dating General Bradshaw's son."

"General—" Shane's head snapped toward me before he too focused on the road again. "You're dating *Bradshaw's* son?"

"Yep. And before you ask, yes, he's legal."

"Well, that's good, but..." Shane whistled and shook his head. "Really? Bradshaw's kid?"

"Yeah." I rubbed my neck with both hands. "And Bradshaw ordered me to stop seeing his son—"

"Seriously?" Shane rolled his eyes. "There's an abuse of authority if I've ever heard one."

"Tell me about it. He basically told me I could stop seeing Connor, or I could find myself on Diego Garcia for a year or two. Which could do a number on my ability to advance."

"Motherfucker," Shane muttered. "So what kind of advice do you need? How to keep him from finding out?"

"Well, no. We've been keeping it on the down-low for a while. I mean, he caught us, but he doesn't know we're still seeing each other."

"High school never ends, does it?" Shane mused.

I laughed halfheartedly. "No, it doesn't." I rested my elbow under the window. "I guess I'm just trying to figure out if I'm being an idiot."

Shane gnawed his thumbnail. "I don't know if I'd word it that way, but you're taking a pretty big risk."

"I know that. But am I an idiot for taking that risk?"

Shane thought for a long moment before he spoke again. "Look, I know as well as anyone what it's like to be with someone you shouldn't. If anyone finds out about Eric and me, we could both be in a world of hurt." He locked eyes with me. "But Connor's a kid. Has he ever even had much of a relationship before?"

"Living under Bradshaw's thumb? Are you kidding?"

"Yeah, that's what I figured. So this is his first time down this road." Shane paused. "You're an Academy grad, right?"

I nodded.

"So you've been planning a military career for a long time. Right?"

Again, I nodded.

"I get how much he probably means to you," Shane said. "And putting your career ahead of someone you care about? Believe me, I understand. I'm one to talk. I'm dating an enlisted guy." He paused and looked at me. "You have to keep your career in mind." He held my gaze, and for a moment, I almost expected a reassuring hand on my arm. "I'm not saying that's easy by any means. I've been struggling with it myself ever since Eric and I started dating."

I swallowed. "So what do I do?"

"I don't know. I really don't." Shane chewed the inside of his cheek. "But the thing is, he's a *kid*."

I raised my eyebrows. *And?*

"Some people get it right the first time," he said, "but most people? They need to fall on their faces a few times. And both of you need a chance to find yourselves and figure out your careers. You're just out of the Academy. He's just out of high school. Do either of you even know who you are yet?"

Being the youngest of four, I was used to my hackles going up when someone implied, because of my age, I didn't know who I was or what I was doing.

This time, though, I had to admit I saw his point. Connor and I were both still figuring out what the fuck we were doing as individuals. What happened if we figured it out and it took us in opposite directions?

Shane went on. "I'm not saying young relationships never work. Some do. Some people really pull it off right out of the gate. You just need to decide how much you're willing to gamble on the possibility that you and Connor are two of those people. It sucks, and it's not remotely fair, but you've got a lot on the line."

I scrubbed a hand over my face. Damn him for making sense. It did make sense too. If we were in our thirties, with our feet under us and some experience behind us, maybe it would be different. But Connor had never had a serious relationship before. I'd had a couple, but even they were nothing to write home about. Nothing I'd ever had any illusions of lasting forever.

Bradshaw could derail—not end, but definitely derail—my career with a few phone calls. I'd worked too goddamned hard for this, spent too much of my life getting to this point, and risking all that for something that was intense now but might flame out in a few months? Stupid. Completely stupid.

I swallowed hard and looked at Shane. "You're probably right."

"I'm sorry," he said. "I really am."

Yeah. Me too.

Chapter Twenty
Connor

When I came home from class, Dad's car was in the driveway. I groaned to myself—having him gone for a week and a half had been *so nice*. Especially since I hadn't had to sneak around with Aiden. My stepmother didn't ask many questions. Unlike my father, she accepted that I was an adult and didn't need permission or oversight to leave the damned house.

I left my books in the car—didn't need to study for anything at the moment, and I'd probably go to the library tomorrow anyway—and went inside.

Dad was in the kitchen, and as soon as I saw him, I knew I was fucked. He gave me that look. Head tilted. Eyes narrowed. Mouth tight. *Fuck.*

He set his iced tea on the counter. "Where were you this weekend?"

My blood turned colder. "What?"

He gave me a look. "Your stepmother said you were gone all weekend. Where were you?"

Casually turning to reach into the refrigerator, I said, "Some friends and I went out to the Keramas to go snorkeling."

"Which friends?"

I turned and glared at him. "Friends who, like me, are old enough to—"

"Cut the crap, Connor," he snapped, making me jump. "Were you or were you not with Ensign Lange this weekend?"

How the fuck...

I gulped, instantly regretting it.

Dad exhaled hard. "We've discussed this."

"Yeah, we have."

He rubbed his forehead. "Connor, I don't think you understand how serious this is."

"And I don't think you understand how serious I am about being with Aiden."

He glared at me. My heart beat faster. I hadn't even thought about what I was saying until the words came out, but now that they had, there was no taking them back.

"So you have been seeing him." It wasn't a question.

My shoulders dropped. I released a breath, and with it the tension that had been winding itself around this secret for the past few weeks. "Yes."

Dad sighed loudly. "Jesus Christ, Connor."

A few years ago, the teenage me would've been worried about how grounded he was going to be. Right then, though, the adult me decided this was horseshit.

I grabbed my keys off the counter. "I'm going out."

"Where?"

"To the fucking library."

"Connor, if you're—"

The door closed and cut him off. I half expected him to come out and order me back into the house like he would've if I'd been a few years younger, but the front door stayed shut.

I got in the car and pulled out of the driveway with no particular destination in mind. I was tempted to go to the library as I'd told my father, but I couldn't focus enough to study, so that was pointless. I also didn't feel like being around people.

Well, with one notable exception.

I pulled out my phone. *You busy tonight?*

A minute or so later.

Nope, not busy. I'm at the Exchange. Want to meet up?

Yes, please. Meet you in the parking lot?

Be out shortly.

I left base housing and drove to the Base Exchange. The parking lot was huge, but after I went down two or three aisles, Aiden's car came into view, and some of the tension melted out of my shoulders. Finally—the one person in the universe who I actually wanted to see.

I parked my car and got into his. As I slid into the passenger seat, Aiden didn't look at me.

"Hey," I said.

This time, he glanced at me, but just long enough for a flicker of a halfhearted smile before he looked out the windshield again. The engine idled, but he didn't put the car in Drive, and he kept his gaze fixed on something outside.

For the second time this afternoon, my blood turned cold.

"You okay?"

Aiden sighed, rubbing a hand over his face. "Yeah. Just...a long day."

Why don't I believe you?

I gnawed my lip. "My, uh, stepmom told my dad I was gone for the weekend."

Aiden's head snapped toward me, and his eyebrows went up. "Did she?"

"Yeah. I blew it off and told him I'd gone out to the Keramas with some friends. He bought it, as far as I can tell." *Liar.*

"Oh. Good." Aiden faced forward again but didn't relax at all.

"What's wrong?" I asked. "You're not you today."

Aiden exhaled, and his shoulders sank as he did. His expression went from bland to downright hurting.

I reached for his knee, and when he flinched away from my touch, my heart dropped. "Aiden." I pulled my hand back. "What's going on?"

He chewed his lower lip. "We, uh, need to talk."

I gulped. "What about?" More than I'd ever been, I was tempted to reach for him—bridge the gap, make some contact—but I could still feel his flinch reverberating through my bones like a *Stay Out* electric shock. I wasn't sure I could take that a second time.

Aiden turned toward me, but he stared at something outside. His jaw was tight, his lips pressed together.

My stomach flipped and twisted. "Just tell—"

"I can't..." He lowered his gaze. "I can't do this, Connor. I'm sorry."

My stomach lurched. "What? What do you mean?"

Sighing, he scrubbed a hand over his face. "I can't keep being the reason things are rough between you and your father."

"That's for him and me to figure out."

"Yeah, but..." He dropped his hand onto the console between us, but still didn't look at me. "He's also got my career by the balls."

I ground my teeth. "So it's not about me and my dad. It's about your career."

Finally, he turned toward me, and, Jesus, he looked exhausted. Dark lines under his eyes, shoulders hunched like he couldn't even hold them up. "I'm not saying this is easy, Connor. It's not." He closed his eyes and shook his head. "It's so not."

"Has it occurred to you that it's hard because it's the wrong decision?"

He swallowed hard. "I've been thinking about that for days."

"And?"

Aiden shook his head and looked out the windshield again. "I'm sorry. I really am."

"Then why..." I couldn't find the words, and I could barely breathe enough to speak anyway.

He focused on something up ahead. "This is your first time—"

"So what? Is there a certain number of times I have to do it before my opinion is valid or I can say it's right or wrong?"

"No, of course not. But most people have to go through a few relationships before they find the right one."

"And what happens if we get it right the first time?" I swallowed hard, trying not to let him see just how panicked I was at the thought of losing him. "Are we supposed to shoot it in the foot and end it just because it's the first time?"

He didn't answer.

I glared at him. "Would you be willing to give it a shot if my dad hadn't threatened your career?"

"Connor..." He exhaled hard.

I rubbed a hand over my face. "Christ..."

"This isn't just *my* future," he said quietly. "If you keep seeing me, that could fuck things up with your dad and get in the way of you finishing school."

I rolled my eyes. "Whatever helps you sleep at night."

Again, he didn't respond.

"You know what? Just...forget it."

I had no idea if he wanted to exchange a few parting words because I didn't give him the chance. I got out of the car, shut the door behind me and didn't look back. Hands shaking and stomach clenched, I got into my own car and headed home.

When I got to the house, I went in as quietly as I could. I felt like a goddamned kid, slipping into my own house past my parents and retreating to my bedroom, but I couldn't concentrate enough to drive anywhere other than from the Exchange to here, and there was nowhere else to go.

In my bedroom, I sank onto the bed.

And I felt nothing.

I didn't cry. I didn't get angry. I didn't feel sick.

I felt...absolutely nothing.

Somewhere under my skin, there were feelings, but they were so far away they may as well have belonged to someone else.

I kept expecting Aiden to call, but my phone stayed silent. And I couldn't understand it. What he'd said in the car, why he'd let me go. This couldn't be how it ended. It wasn't right. It didn't make sense. Something had happened between us, and it was too deep to be dismissed like this, and now that he was gone, I didn't know what to think. Feel. Do.

I'd known for a while that I was in love with Aiden, but now that he was gone? Fuck. Even now, as much as I wanted to resent him for choosing his career over me, I couldn't. On some level, I was angry. Mostly, I was numb. I felt empty.

And I should have hated him but, God, I loved him.

Chapter Twenty-One
Aiden

I'd made a huge mistake. A massive one.

For a solid week, that was all I could think about. I couldn't concentrate on work. I sure as shit couldn't look General Bradshaw in the eye.

I had seriously fucked up.

Question was, which was the mistake? Breaking up with Connor, or hooking up with him in the first place?

I pushed aside the paperwork I was supposed to be focusing on. Why I'd bothered to work on it at all, I had no idea. I was lucky I'd been able to put my shoes on this morning, never mind comprehend a threat analysis detailing some concerns about Kadena's southernmost fence line.

I needed to talk to someone. Now.

I would have given my right arm for a chance to take Shane up on his open-door policy, but this wasn't a good time for him. Rumors were already flying all over the building about the altercation between him and Commander Morris the other night. I thought it might've been just bullshit, but Morris was gone—permanently, by the sound of it—and when I caught a glimpse of Shane, he looked like he hadn't slept in weeks and had one hell of a bruise on the side of his face. Secretly, I hoped he'd whooped Morris's ass. He probably hadn't, not if he still had a job, but I wouldn't have been sad to find out that the homophobic son of a bitch had taken a few hits.

The last thing Shane needed was my bullshit, but, God, I needed that lifeline. That open office door. Someone who got it. He'd been the one to convince me that I was playing with fire if I stayed with Connor, and I needed him to remind me of everything he'd told me at the barbecue. What was at stake. Why I'd be an idiot to risk my career for something that wouldn't last.

I wanted to believe he was right. I needed to believe that ending things with Connor had been a necessary, painful evil.

But I didn't.

And I still had work to do. Breakup or not, idiot or not, I had shit that needed to get done, so I pulled up the PowerPoint presentation I was supposed to give at Island Indoc next week. The slides were fine, I thought, but the brass always found something that needed some adjustments. I had the slides, I had the notes they'd given me, and, nope, couldn't concentrate on that either. I could barely make out the words on the screen or the notes, never mind figure out how to tweak the slides for whatever reason I felt possessed to tweak them.

I let my face fall into my hands. Christ. I was fucking useless today. Sitting in my office, I was about to go out of my mind, but I was afraid to step out for so much as a cup of coffee because I didn't want to run into Bradshaw. Did he know yet? Was he one of those fathers who'd hate me for dating his son, but kill me for dumping him?

I rested my elbows on my desk and rubbed both hands over my face. This shit would get easier, wouldn't it? It had to. It wasn't like I'd had much choice. Connor and I couldn't make this work.

Could we?

Fuck.

Yeah. Definitely useless for the day.

I called Captain Warren and told him I needed to take off at two so I could take care of some personal things. He didn't mind—he probably had a tee time himself—so at a few minutes before two, I slipped out of my office and left.

Once I was off the base, I went home and changed out of my uniform. Then, without really thinking about it, I got in the car and hit the road again. I turned onto Highway 329, and I drove.

No direction in mind, no particular destination. I just drove.

I just...drove.

Through one of the little towns outside Kadena. Past farms and shops and sugarcane fields. Without really thinking about it, I followed the signs onto the expressway. On autopilot, I grabbed a ticket from the toll machine, then accelerated up the ramp and merged with the sparse traffic. I ignored the speed limit, as I always did, and flew up the expressway, pretending I didn't feel a conspicuous void beside me where Connor used to sit.

I drove way too fast, and before I knew it, I'd reached the end of the expressway, just outside of Nago. I stopped at the tollbooth, paid the toll and continued up the highway. Still no destination in mind, but I kept heading north.

There was almost no one out on the highway, and the few cars out here were observing the speed limit about as well as I was. A souped-up sports car blew by me, and I couldn't resist applying a little more pressure to the accelerator. The engine whined, and the seawall and tsunami breaks and tiny towns whipped past me as I continued toward destination unknown.

I needed to stop somewhere and just think, but I couldn't get away from us. Every familiar inch of this island was something he'd shown me. Something I'd experienced with him. Or something we'd sworn we'd visit soon. A cliff where we'd sat and talked. A beach where we'd made out, talked, fucked. A restaurant where he'd introduced me to the cuisine he knew so well. The resort where I'd realized way too much about us to have done what I did the other night.

And as I continued past Nago, continuing north on 329, I realized with a sinking heart where I'd been heading on autopilot. I wanted to turn around and drive as fast and as far in the opposite direction as this tiny island would let me, but I didn't. Though I knew it would hurt, I kept going. I followed the signs. And when one of those signs told me to pull off the freeway, I did, and I kept following them.

All the way to Hiji Falls.

With my heart in my throat, I parked in the familiar parking lot. Two spaces down from where Connor had parked that day, I remembered way too clearly.

I started up the familiar trail. I followed the familiar staircases up and down, completely numb except for my aching legs. It seemed like a million years ago that I'd been rattled and scared because of that fucking Marine, walking up this trail with the irrational fear that he'd come around the next corner and add to the stitches and bruises on my face. For that matter, I'd become so accustomed to Connor in my life, it was weird to even imagine that I'd been in a gay bar, flirting with anyone else in the first place. Once we'd started seeing each other, he'd become a fixture in my world, something that may as well have been there from day one.

And now he was gone.

And I was here.

And I didn't know why.

What the fuck *was* I doing here? Rubbing salt in an open wound?

I couldn't talk myself out of it, though. Even as I questioned just what the fuck I was doing here, my feet kept moving, taking me deeper into the thick forest.

When I'd come up here the first time, I'd been irrationally terrified that the Marine who'd roughed me up would be waiting for me around the next bend. Now, every corner, curve and staircase gave me the same empty feeling. Connor wouldn't be waiting. We wouldn't run into each other.

He wasn't here. He was gone.

And never was that point clearer than when I made it up to the falls at the end of the trail. There was no one here. No other tourists. No locals. No Americans. No beautiful, shirtless Connor standing waist-deep in the cool water.

I sat on top of one of the boulders and stared out at the pool. There wasn't another person out here, no sound except for the birds and the water cascading over the rocks.

Coming back here hurt way more than it should have if this was just something I could let go of and move on. If it really was a mistake to hook up with him in the first place.

That part definitely wasn't the mistake. As the water fell into the pool and the birds chirped overhead, and there *wasn't* a gorgeous dark-haired kid disturbing the mostly calm pool by striding across it toward me while I stared like a dumbstruck idiot, the truth was unavoidable. Everything from that moment to the other night had been right. It had been perfect.

And what did I do?

I fucked it up. And now, sitting here and letting the pain sink its teeth all the way in, I couldn't even begin to convince myself that this was how it was supposed to be. I wasn't supposed to be up here at Hiji Falls without Connor. I wasn't supposed to be anywhere without him.

Because I loved him.

My own thought made me wince. I was, wasn't I? I was in love with Connor. It didn't matter that he was the general's kid, or that he was young, or that a relationship with him might land me on Diego Garcia or derail my career. I loved him.

When I'd broken up with him, it had been painful but made sense at the time. Now? It didn't make any sense at all. I wasn't giving up a fling with a kid for the sake of the career I'd worked my ass off to build.

In the name of rank and strategy, I'd given up the love of my life.

It was that fucking simple.

Chapter Twenty-Two
Connor

A full week had passed since I'd stepped out of Aiden's car, and I'd never hurt so bad in my life. The numbness was gone. The shock had worn off. Now every song I'd ever heard about breakups made sense. Now I got it. And I wished I didn't.

At least I'd been able to study. Throwing myself into my classes had given me something to do, something to focus on, but the second I stepped away from a book, I was a wreck again. I didn't even leave the house for three days straight.

Today, the walls had started closing in around me, so I'd gotten in the car and driven until I found a remote beach in the middle of nowhere. I left my shoes in the car, wandered down to the sand and sat a few feet above the high-tide line.

I pushed my toes into the sand and stared out at the turquoise water. Places like this usually brought me a sense of peace. Any time my dad and I fought, or I was frustrated with school, or I'd had one of those god-awful Skype sessions with my mother, I drove until I found a beach. Then I'd sit there and let the ocean relax me. It didn't solve the problem, but it helped settle me.

Today? Nothing.

Especially since every beach had Aiden's name all over it. The beaches on this island were all different—white sand, black rocks, coarse sand, fine sand—but any place where water met land was Aiden. Walking together. Talking together. Watching sunsets. Kissing like it was the only thing either of us wanted to do. And the sex...

I shivered, but it was less a pleasant reaction and more like a nauseated shudder. Maybe someday those memories would turn me on, but right now all they did was make me think of who I didn't have anymore.

Leaning forward, I pressed my fingers into my temples and closed my eyes. For the billionth time, I tried to make sense of everything. Maybe if I could rationalize things and put them into some kind of order, then I could move on.

Except I *had* made sense of it. Everything was already in order. I just couldn't accept it. I couldn't grasp that Aiden really had dumped me to save his career. It made perfect sense, and any idiot would've seen it coming, but that didn't make it hurt any less.

I kneaded the sand with my toes, digging past the hot grains on top to the cool, damp ones below.

I'd told myself all along that I'd never ask Aiden to choose between me and his career. Never. I'd heard those battles between my parents, and I would never put someone in the position my mother had put my father in time and time again. And I'd told him from the start that I'd understand if he needed to walk away for the sake of his career, but that was before I'd felt this much for him. Back when we were just a couple of guys flirting and—eventually—fucking, and there were no feelings involved yet.

And while I would never have *asked* him to choose, I had to admit, when he did choose, it hurt like hell.

What was he supposed to do, Connor?

He'd been working for years to get to this point. He had an entire career ahead of him. Did he really have a choice?

But it still hurt to let him go. Or rather, it still hurt when he let me go.

And now that the shock had worn off and I'd spent some time thinking about things a little more clearly, the pieces started falling together. It didn't just hurt that he'd left.

I was pissed. Fucking pissed.

If there was one thing I hated—especially given my living situation—it was being treated like a child. Having someone make a decision for me. I was stuck living with my dad for the time being, but goddammit, I was a fucking adult. I didn't need someone telling me that I couldn't possibly know what I wanted out of a relationship, or that I was too inexperienced to know how I felt about someone. Or that our relationship wasn't worth keeping because it was my first and by default wouldn't work out anyway.

Fuck that.

Fuck Aiden.

I sniffed a few times and blinked until my vision was clear. Staring out at the ocean, I didn't even fight the anger swelling in my chest.

And damn if this view didn't remind me of him. So did the hot sand under my feet. And the sound of the tide rolling in. And the humidity on my neck and the wind brushing the palm trees behind me.

"Fuck," I said through my teeth and swiped at my eyes.

I couldn't deal with this. I also couldn't escape it.

I sat up. I couldn't escape it unless...

No, I didn't want to do that.

But like Aiden didn't have a choice where our relationship was concerned, I didn't see any choice where my future was concerned. This was what I needed to do.

I stood, brushing the sand off my shorts, and headed back to my car to drive back to Kadena. Passing through all the familiar scenery, I couldn't help the lump that kept rising in my throat. It wasn't just over Aiden this time. I'd made a decision, and every palm tree, every Family Mart, every set of Shi Shi dogs made that decision a little harder.

But I'd made up my mind.

I parked in my usual spot, killed the engine but didn't get out right away. Holding on to the steering wheel, I took a few breaths to compose myself. Then I went inside.

My dad was in the living room, reading something on his iPad. He looked at me but didn't say anything.

"Dad." I swallowed. "Can we talk?"

He looked up from the iPad. "What about?"

I sat in the chair across from his. "College. Me living here."

Dad set his tablet on the cushion beside him. "All right."

I folded my hands and tried not to fidget, which was even harder now that he was staring at me. Finally, I cleared my throat. "I want to leave Okinawa."

"Leave?" He stared at me. "When?"

"As soon as I can." I forced back the lump trying to rise in my throat. "If I have to take out some student loans or get a couple of jobs, fine. I might even take a year off and work to save some money but I just... I need to go."

"Connor." He sighed. "There's a reason we have this arrangement. I don't want you starting out neck-deep in debt."

"Then what should I do?"

"Keep doing what you've been doing. You've only got a couple of years left on your degree."

"And I can't stay here. I just... Dad, I can't do this. I *need* to get out on my own."

He looked at me for almost a minute before he said, "Is this about Ensign Lange?"

I winced and dropped my gaze. "Partly."

"Partly?"

"Look, you don't want me dating military guys, and just about every guy I could possibly date on this island is military." I shook my head. "I'm tired of not being able to have a relationship."

"I'm assuming this means you're not seeing him anymore." He was probably relieved as fuck, but there wasn't any smugness in his voice.

I tried to ignore the ache in my throat. "We didn't have much choice."

Dad flinched. He picked up his iPad again but didn't turn it on, just ran his thumb along the edge like he needed something to do with his hands. I knew the feeling. After a while, he said, "I know it's difficult being on an island like this without being able to date military men." He looked at me. "But you know I never did this to make you miserable."

My throat ached, and I gritted my teeth. "I know. I understand why you're doing it, but..." Shaking my head again, I avoided his eyes. "I want to meet someone. I'm tired of—" My voice cracked. I cleared my throat again. "There's just no way I can do this for two more years."

My father was silent for a long time. Then he nodded slowly. "If that's what you want to do, then I'll help you make the arrangements."

"Thank you."

"Do you have any place in mind?"

"Not...not yet. I'll look around, maybe figure out which college I want to transfer to."

He chewed his lip. "You do realize that if you apply for student loans as my dependent, you'll be turned down because of my income."

I nodded. "I know. I wasn't planning to apply as a dependent."

His eyebrows arched, but he didn't object. "The job market isn't so good over there. You know that, right?"

"Yeah."

"Well, to get you on your feet, I suppose we can work out a loan of sorts. Something you can pay back after you graduate." He wagged a finger at me. "One of the conditions will be that you finish your degree within the next three years, though."

As much as the gesture annoyed me, the offer of a loan was a huge relief, so I just nodded and whispered, "Thanks."

After another long silence, he said, "I'm going to miss you, son, but if this is what you need to do..."

"It is."

He was quiet for a moment. "I can also make some arrangements with your grandmother. See if they'll let you stay with them while you decide what you're doing."

"Really?"

Dad nodded. "We'll work something out. Like I said, a loan or something until you're good."

"Thanks."

"You're welcome. I'm sorry you're leaving, though."

"Me too."

There was so much I needed to do. Figure out where I wanted to live. Find a source of income. Start packing and fill out paperwork. Sell my car.

But just making the decision had taken all the energy I had left today.

I went outside and sat in one of the chairs on the back porch. From here, I had a gorgeous view of the ocean just beyond the strip of buildings outside Kadena's fence. A short drive in any direction would take me to one of a million of my favorite places in the world. Castles. Shops that sold cool shit I couldn't find anywhere else. Restaurants. The beach.

I winced, all the air leaving my lungs in a single rush. I'd never be able to look at a beach again without thinking about Aiden. Hell, who was I kidding? There was no place on this island that didn't say his name to me.

Still, I didn't want to leave this place. This had been home since I was a teenager.

But I couldn't keep living under my father's thumb, and I couldn't stomach being on this tiny island where every time I turned around, Aiden might be standing there.

I had no idea where I'd eventually go.

I couldn't think of any place far enough from here.

Chapter Twenty-Three
Aiden

I gripped the wheel with both hands and reminded myself with every single kilometer that this was the right thing to do. It might send my career down in flames, but to hell with it.

Three times this week, I'd made this drive. The first time, I'd almost made it to my destination. The second and third, I'd lost my nerve within a kilometer of Kadena's gate.

If I didn't make it this time, then it wasn't going to happen, so I kept my foot on the accelerator and my hands on the wheel, hovering a few clicks above the base speed limit and hoping no one from Security Forces caught me. Getting pulled over would be a convenient excuse to bail on this, and I wasn't bailing. I couldn't. I hadn't had a good night's sleep in the two solid weeks since I'd broken up with Connor, and I couldn't concentrate on anything but this.

Now or never, and never wasn't an option.

Stomach twisting into knots and heart pounding in my chest, I drove past the entrance to officer housing. My sweaty palms tried to slide on the wheel, but I was holding it tight enough that I didn't lose my grip.

General Bradshaw's house came into view. No turning back now.

I parked in front of the closed garage door. Connor's car was nowhere in sight. That was disappointing but didn't make me turn back. He wasn't the one I'd come here to see.

On my way up the walk, I swallowed a few times to keep the nausea from getting the best of me. I wasn't turning back, not even if I freaked myself out so badly I got sick. I was doing this. Today. Now.

At the door, I paused. Took a deep breath. Set my shoulders back. And knocked.

A moment later, a pretty Japanese woman opened the door. "Yes?"

I cleared my throat. "I'm here to see General Bradshaw."

"Of course." She bowed and gestured for me to come in. I toed off my shoes and left them in one of the neat shelves beside the door, and the woman—Bradshaw's wife, I assumed—led me into the living room. "Wait here."

"Thank you."

She disappeared down the hall.

While I waited, I fought the urge to pace across the cream-colored carpet. I didn't want Bradshaw seeing my nerves. Hell, I didn't want to even acknowledge them myself—the second I accepted I was really *that* nervous would be the second I couldn't talk myself into staying.

Footsteps came down the hall. They were soft and shoeless, but definitely heavier than the woman who'd greeted me.

Here we go.

I steeled myself and turned around as Bradshaw appeared.

He was dressed in civvies—khaki shorts and a golf shirt—but he was no less intimidating now than in his uniform. Surprise flickered across his expression, quickly replaced by irritation. "Ensign. This is...unexpected."

"I know. I...didn't want to do this at the office."

His eyes narrowed. "Do what?"

"I want to talk to you." I gulped. "About Connor."

No surprise registered this time. "We've discussed all we need to discuss. The subject is—"

"We haven't."

His eyebrows jumped.

Thank God he wasn't in uniform, or all my training would have had me cowering under his rank. Even in civvies, I struggled to ignore the huge gap between our pay grades and all the ways this could bite me in the ass.

I set my shoulders back. "Sir, with all due respect, I'm not going to stop seeing your son."

His posture stiffened. "I beg your pardon, *Ensign*?"

I refused to flinch. Not visibly, anyway. "I'm not going to stop seeing your son. Sir."

Slowly, menacingly, he folded his arms across his broad chest. "You are way out of line here."

"Maybe I am." *Oh, I* so *am.* "But, again, with all due respect, this isn't about you."

His eyebrows rose even higher and he stood even straighter. "It isn't about me? Connor is my son. It's—"

"He's an adult."

"He's barely twenty, Ensign!"

"And that makes him an adult."

"Adult or not, he's still my son." General Bradshaw came closer, looming over me. "And as long as he lives under my roof—"

"Then he can live with me."

The general's eyebrows shot up. "Come again?"

"You heard me." I swallowed. "If you throw him out, then he can stay with me. Is that what you want?"

His lips thinned into a bleached line. "I'm not throwing my son out of the house."

"But you'll still forbid him from seeing me?"

"I'm not forbidding *him* from seeing *you.*"

I willed my knees not to shake. "Understood. And go ahead and string me up if you want to, sir. Make your phone calls and have me sent to Bahrain or Diego Garcia." I threw up my hands. "At this point, I really don't care what you do to me. I'm in love with your son."

My own words rattled me to the core. Not the insubordination, not the fact that I was speaking like this to a general. I was in love with Connor. I'd known it, but now that I'd said it, my composure wavered. God, what had I done?

Still glaring at me, Bradshaw didn't move or speak.

I squared my shoulders. "I'm in love with him, sir. You can send me off to some remote island. Whatever you have to do. But the only one who's going to keep me away is Connor."

His eyes started to narrow again, and I could feel his tirade coming like a storm rolling in.

Before he could speak, though, I continued. "Quite honestly, you might not even have to worry about him dating me. I screwed up. I ended it. I was afraid of what you might do to my career, and I was afraid of what might happen to him, so I...I ended it. And it was the worst mistake I've ever made." I set my shoulders back, pretending my stomach wasn't an even bigger ball of nerves than it had been when I'd arrived. "So he might not even want to speak to me, let alone see me, but...he needs to know how I feel, and if he'll have me, I..." I gritted my teeth, refusing to let this man see me lose control. "I love him, and if he'll have me, I want him back. Regardless of what you decide to do to me."

Bradshaw still didn't speak. He regarded me silently for a long moment, the hostility in his expression faltering just slightly in favor of...of something else. Something I couldn't quite put my finger on.

When he finally spoke, his voice was quiet and as unreadable as his expression. "He's *twenty*, Ensign." Bradshaw shook his head. "As far as I know, he's never even had a boyfriend. How in the—"

"So what?"

"So..." The general sighed. "I..." Then he paused. "Connor."

I furrowed my brow, unsure why he'd just said his son's name.

After a moment, I realized he wasn't looking at me. He was looking past me.

Slowly, I turned around, and my breath caught as I realized Connor was standing in the doorway. Arms folded tight across his Metallica T-shirt, he leaned against the frame and watched us, his expression unreadable.

My heart jumped into my throat. How much had he heard?

For a long moment, no one moved. No one spoke.

Without a word, Connor shouldered himself off the doorframe. My knees shook as he crossed the room.

He stopped an arm's length away. No one made a sound. No one moved.

Connor searched my eyes. I swore I could hear his thoughts as he did, and hoped to God he could hear mine.

Did you mean what you said?

Every word.

Then he took another step forward and threw his arms around me. I released my breath as I hugged him back, closing my eyes and burying my face against his neck. Just catching his familiar scent was enough to make my eyes sting. He was really here. He hadn't shoved me away, hadn't told me to go fuck myself. We weren't back on solid ground, not yet, but this was a damned good start.

"God, Connor, I am so sorry for—"

"I love you."

I held him tighter. "I love you too." I wanted to kiss him, to taste him and make sure he was real, but I couldn't let go of him. "I'm so sorry."

"Don't." He stroked my hair. "Just don't." He loosened his embrace, and as I drew back, I touched my forehead to his.

"I didn't realize you were here." I ran my fingertips down his cheek. "Your car wasn't outside, so I—"

"I sold it."

Something in his voice gave me pause. "Connor..."

Eyes still down, he whispered, "I'm leaving Okinawa."

My heart dropped into my feet. "Leaving?"

"Yeah." He looked at me again. "I've already started the paperwork and transfer screenings." He chewed his lip. Barely whispering, he added, "I fly out in two weeks."

If my heart could've dropped any farther, it would've.

"I'm sorry," he said. "I...I just couldn't stay here. I'm applying to transfer to some stateside colleges and staying with some relatives until I get everything together." He shook his head. "I'm sorry, Aiden. I—"

"It's nothing to apologize for." I wrapped my arms around him again. "And we can still make it work. If you want to do this, we can. There are flights from here all the time."

Connor still held on to me, but his embrace loosened a little, and his shoulders sank slightly. I swore I could feel him slipping away.

We can *make this work, Connor. Please don't give up on me.*

A gruff cough startled me and reminded me we weren't alone. My blood turned cold, and I straightened, certain Bradshaw was about to lose his shit. Connor and I released each other, inching apart as if that would somehow negate anything.

But Bradshaw looked at his son, and in a gentler tone than I'd ever heard from him, he said, "It's not too late, Connor."

Connor shifted his weight. "But all the paperwork has started and—"

"I can make some calls." The general's eyes flicked toward me, then back to his son. "If this is what you want, then..."

Connor looked up at me.

I touched his face. "It's up to you."

"Do you want me to stay?" he asked so softly I barely heard him.

"Absolutely." I ran my thumb along his cheekbone. "But if you need to go, I'll understand. We can...we can still—"

"I want to stay." Connor turned to his father. "It's really not too late?"

"No. I can make some calls." Bradshaw glanced back and forth between us. "Is this what you want, Connor?"

Connor's gaze darted toward me, then back to his father. "What about all the fraternization stuff? I thought—"

Bradshaw let out a long breath, his shoulders sinking, and I swore he seemed to age ten years in a few seconds. "It's still a risk. For both of us. But now that I've seen that you're willing to leave the island over this, and after Ensign Lange was willing to confront me, I..." He shook his head. "I can't keep you from something that makes you both happy." He looked me right in the eye, then looked at Connor. "Is this what you want, son?"

Nodding, Connor laced his fingers between mine. "Yes."

Bradshaw stared at our joined hands. I wanted so badly to rub my thumb along the side of Connor's, but I was afraid even the slightest movement would turn the general from this weirdly subdued version back to the volatile asshole who didn't want me anywhere near his son.

"All right." Bradshaw gave a single nod and shifted his weight. "I'll make the calls tomorrow."

"Thank you." Connor let go of my hand, and embraced his father tightly.

"I'm sorry, son," General Bradshaw said quietly. "You know I only—"

"I know. It's okay."

Bradshaw let him go, and then he turned to me. After a moment, the general extended his hand. "Ensign."

"General." I shook his hand.

Without releasing his grip, he set his jaw and held my gaze. "I'm sure I don't have to tell you that it's best if things are discreet around the office."

I nodded. "Of course."

"Good. Good." He released my hand and glanced at Connor. "I'll, uh, leave you two alone, then."

"Thanks, Dad," Connor said.

Bradshaw looked at Connor, then at me, and then stepped out of the room. As soon as he was gone, I exhaled and leaned against the back of the couch.

Connor laughed. "My dad doesn't make you nervous, does he?"

"Uh, well, he definitely did when I was on my way over here."

Connor's expression turned more serious, but he didn't say anything.

"I'm sorry it took so long," I whispered, sliding an arm around his waist. "I've almost come over here a few times, I was just...scared."

He laughed again, but halfheartedly. "My dad's a scary dude when he wants to be."

"No, it wasn't because of him." I ran my fingers through Connor's hair. "It was because of you."

Connor tensed. "What?"

"I hurt you," I said. "You had every right to be pissed at me, and I was scared to death you'd turn me away." I leaned in and kissed his forehead. "God, I am so sorry, Connor."

"You're back now." He met my eyes. "That's all I care about. You're back."

"I am." I cradled his face in both hands. "And I love you."

He smiled. "I love you too."

I held his gaze for a long moment, just drinking in the fact that we'd found our way back to each other. Then I leaned in slowly, and as I tilted my head, he lifted his chin, and when our lips met, I damn near had to push him up against the wall just to keep from melting to the floor.

When we broke the kiss, I was shaking.

"So what do we do now?" He smirked. "Can't really...with my parents home..."

I laughed. "No, I guess we can't." Nodding toward the door, I added, "I'm parked outside. Do you want to, um, go grab a bite to eat?" I paused, heart thundering. "I mean, if you're not studying or anything."

"Not really hungry right now." Connor reached for my face. "But I can think of someplace else we could go."

Chapter Twenty-Four
Connor

Even sliding into the passenger seat of Aiden's car was a relief. Like things were finally back to normal. Half an hour ago, I'd never wanted to see him again, but then I'd heard his voice downstairs. I'd listened in, and he'd said all those things, and I'd believed him. Every word. Because he'd said them when he didn't think I was listening. He'd poured it all out to my father, knowing full well there could be unpleasant consequences and thinking all along I wouldn't hear it, never mind take him back if I did.

But here we were, and the world felt like it was spinning the right way again.

As he started the engine, I touched his leg. "That took some balls, coming at him like that. I can't even stand up to him the way you did."

Aiden laughed, his cheeks coloring a little. "Now you know why it took me so long to do it."

I laughed too and took his hand. "I'm glad you did."

"Me too." He slipped his fingers between mine. "Were you really leaving in two weeks?"

"Probably sooner." I watched his thumb rub the side of my hand. "I was going to take a Space-A flight out next week. Once we had everything sorted out."

Aiden exhaled. "Wow. And you were leaving because of..."

Nodding, I avoided his eyes. "I know it sounds stupid to up and leave over this, but it was just going to happen again. With any other guy I met. And..." I made myself meet his gaze again. "I didn't want to meet any other guys. I wanted you."

Aiden touched my face. "I am so sorry. I—"

"Stop apologizing," I whispered. "I know why you did it. I understand." Smiling, I ran my fingers through his hair. "And you're back, and I'm not going anywhere now. I don't care about anything else."

"Thank God." He leaned across the console to kiss me. "I missed you so much."

"I missed you too." I held the side of his neck and kissed him again, pushing his lips apart with my tongue. A low groan vibrated against my hand, and the kiss deepened as we pulled each other closer.

It was Aiden who finally broke away and said, "Maybe we should find someplace a little more private."

"Good idea." I raised an eyebrow. "I can think of one place."

He held my gaze.

Then he grinned. So did I.

And he put the car in Reverse.

Somehow we made it all the way to Aiden's apartment and all the way up the stairs without giving in, but about the time we made it to his floor, we went from *almost there* to *fuck it, close enough.* I pushed him up against the railing and kissed him hard, and he didn't fight me, didn't tell me to just be patient for a few more steps. Oh God, no. He grabbed on and kissed me like his life depended on it.

We stumbled a little, and before I knew it, my back was against the wall, Aiden pinning me there with his body, both hands cupping my neck as he kissed me hard. I gripped his shirt, his hair, his neck—anything I could grab hold of—and when he pressed his hips into mine, I pushed back, rubbing and grinding against him and wishing like hell the friction would just melt our clothes away and leave nothing between us but skin.

I didn't even care that we were outside, exposed and in the open. I desperately wanted to get him naked and relieve this hard-on that was about to drive me insane. More than that, though, just holding on to him and tasting his kiss again was an even bigger relief than any orgasm would be. I'd given up on ever touching him again, on him ever wanting me again, but here he was and here I was. Part of me even wanted to break down in tears because I realized even more than before how much it had hurt to be away from him, and how much of a relief it was to have him and to know he loved me.

I slid my hands under his shirt, sighing when my palms met his hot skin, but we didn't move and didn't break this long, frantic kiss. His erection ground against mine, and my fingers dug into his back, and we were going to wind up fucking right then and there if—

Aiden suddenly broke away, touching his forehead to mine and panting hard against my lips. "We should get inside."

"I don't want to move."

"Neither do I." He kissed me again, briefly this time. "But there's lube in there."

Our eyes met, and we separated abruptly. He picked his keys up off the concrete—I hadn't even heard them fall. His hands shook as he tried to unlock the door, and even though I really wanted to touch him, I didn't, because that would've just distracted him that much more.

We stumbled through the front door, tangled up and tripping over each other on the way down the short hall to the bedroom. We'd almost always been slow and gentle, but not this time. How we made it into the bedroom without just dropping to the floor and fucking, I'd never know.

But we did, and, gripping the front of my shirt, Aiden dragged me down onto the bed on top of him. My collar dug into the back of my neck, but I didn't care. It was hard to care about anything when Aiden was under me and kissing me like that.

He held me tighter and then rolled me onto my back. As he kissed my neck, he said, "I want to fuck you."

Just thinking about him inside me brought a moan out of me. "Please."

"On your back." He kissed me once more before getting up. "So I can see you."

"My favorite."

We exchanged grins, and while he pulled the lube out of the nightstand drawer, I put a pillow under my hips. He teased me with his fingers until I'd relaxed a little, but he didn't draw it out this time.

As Aiden's cock slid into me and my vision turned white, I gripped his arms. He slid his arms under me and hooked his fingers over my shoulders. The leverage, the angle—Jesus, it felt amazing.

As desperate as we both were, Aiden moved slowly inside me, and I couldn't bring myself to beg him for more. I still couldn't quite believe this was happening, that we'd found our way back to each other like this, and I was sure if I made a sound I'd wake up and it would all be a fantasy.

"You feel so good," he whispered, his whole body trembling as if his slow, smooth motions took every bit of exertion he could muster.

"So do you." I dragged my fingers down his back, feeling his muscles moving beneath his skin as he moved in me. "God, Aiden..."

He whimpered softly in my ear and shuddered against me, shoulders quivering as his breath rushed past my neck. "Fuck, I can't..."

"Come," I whispered, rocking my hips to encourage his. "I want you to—"

He shuddered, and then he was all the way inside me, shaking and moaning, and, Jesus, he was gorgeous like that.

Then he collapsed, arms trembling under him as he tried to hold himself up. "Holy. Shit."

"My thoughts exactly." I pulled him all the way down and kissed him.

After a moment, Aiden pulled out and lifted himself up. I started to get up too, but he pushed me back down.

"Where do you think you're going? We're not done yet." Eyes locked on mine, he held himself up on one arm and reached between us with the other. "We're not done until you come."

His fingers closed around my dick. I knew it was coming but gasped anyway and thrust into his hand.

"Like that?" he asked and squeezed a little harder.

"Yeah. Fuck. Oh my God..." I tried to kiss him, but his hand slid over the head of my cock, and I forgot how. I fell back to the bed, murmuring curses.

"You look amazing." Aiden bit his lip and stroked me a little harder. "I love watching you like this."

"You're not...watching..." Fingers digging into his shoulders, I fucked his fist as he took me closer and closer. "You're *making* me like this."

"I know," he whispered. "And I fucking love it."

That was all it took. My eyes rolled back and my toes curled and I lost it. I called out something—his name? More curses?

Fuck if I knew—and Aiden kept stroking me, kept whispering to me, until I came down. My cock was on the verge of being hypersensitive, and he stopped a second before I'd have asked him to.

We cleaned ourselves up and, as we usually did, climbed back into bed and wrapped up in each other under the sheet.

"It's so good to have you back," he said.

"Likewise."

"I'm sorry. For walking away." Aiden smoothed my hair, that gentle touch I loved so much. "I don't know if it makes a difference, but doing that hurt like hell. I just got scared and didn't see any other way, but I never wanted—"

I cut him off with a kiss. "I know."

"I have no idea what's going to happen." He kissed my forehead. "This could flame out in a few months, or it could last. I don't know. I just... I don't know." He kissed me again, on the mouth this time. "But I can't... I just—"

I silenced him with another kiss. "My parents dated for five years before they got married, and they divorced five years after that. Dad and Hitomi got married six weeks after they met, and they're coming on ten years." I shrugged. "Anything's possible."

"Yeah, anything's possible."

"Who knows?" I said. "Maybe we get to be the lucky ones who get it right."

Aiden smiled. "Maybe. I hope so."

"Me too."

He lifted my chin with two fingers. "The only thing I know is that I love you."

"I love you too." I let him draw me in for a light kiss. "And I'm not leaving."

Aiden met my eyes. "Neither am I."

And, my God, I hoped he meant it.

Because I did.

Epilogue
Aiden

About two years later

Trust Eric and Shane to get married during the damned monsoon.

The grass was damp, and the humidity was way up, but at least it hadn't actually rained today. The last week had been off and on torrential downpours, and everyone in the office had been taking bets about whether the guys would have to move their wedding to some place indoors.

I didn't know what they'd sacrificed to which deity, but the weather cooperated today. The precipitation, anyway. The heat was present and accounted for. Fortunately, I'd long ago adapted to the heat of the island, and at least my dress uniform was relatively thin. Considering I had to walk to the top of Katsuren Castle in it, I was grateful.

As Connor and I started the walk up the hill from the parking lot, I saw a few of the guys from my command, including Captain Warren. I was worried someone might get on my case for wearing inappropriate shoes with my uniform, but as I looked around, I realized everyone else was doing the same thing—dress shoes in hand, sneakers or boots for the climb. Apparently we'd all had the same idea.

Shoes aside, I wasn't worried about anyone from work seeing us. The very few people here from the command already knew about our relationship, and all understood the need for discretion. Captain Warren had even shifted things around a little so I wasn't working directly with Bradshaw anymore.

Basically, I gave the paperwork to Warren, and he passed them on to Bradshaw. The less we interacted directly, the less it could be called a conflict of interest.

There weren't a lot of tourists out today, and what few there were definitely noticed the number of uniformed American military personnel heading up to the castle and making their way to the top level. A few took pictures of us—trust Eric and Shane to stop and pose for them too.

We continued upward.

The uppermost level of Katsuren Castle was crowded with military and civilians alike. There couldn't have been more than twenty-five people, but the small stone enclosure wouldn't have held much more than that.

As we waited for the ceremony to start, Connor slipped his hand around my elbow. "I think I've figured out how the Navy came up with their uniforms."

"How's that?"

Squinting, he glanced at me. "The white and gold blind the enemy."

I laughed and slid my arm around his waist. "Yeah. That's it." I gestured toward the two grooms as they stepped into the enclosure. "And it looks pretty damned good on both of them."

Shane had been an officer all along, but Eric had been enlisted up until fairly recently. He'd gone through the limited duty officer program, though, and gotten his commission, which was why he was wearing whites a lot like Shane's. And why the two of them could finally go public with their relationship.

Which was why we were here, of course.

"Hey, you made it!" Eric grinned as they came toward us.

"Of course we did." I saluted both of them sharply, and they returned it.

Then I shook hands with each in turn. As Shane extended his hand, he said, "Glad you could make it, Lieutenant."

"I wouldn't miss it." I shook his hand. "Congratulations."

He slid his other arm around Eric's waist. "Thanks."

They continued mingling with their guests, and we did as well. While Connor was talking to someone, I bowed out and wandered over to the wall to look out at the island below.

Someone appeared beside me. I thought it was Connor, but when I turned, it was Shane.

"Oh hey," I said.

"Hey." He touched my shoulder. "Listen, I..." He glanced at Connor, then back at me. "Seeing you guys here, I gotta say, Aiden, I'm sorry for suggesting that you and he go your separate ways. Obviously, I was wrong."

"You've apologized a hundred times." I laughed. "It's okay."

He frowned. "I know, but I still feel like shit for it. Could've really fucked up something good for you, you know?"

I shrugged. "Don't worry about it. To be honest, I think we both needed to face down the fact that I was gambling with my career on a relationship that might not work. We needed to consider that, and we hadn't until you mentioned it. And we came out of it knowing damn well we were willing to take the gamble."

Shane held my gaze for a moment, then finally nodded. "Well, I'm glad I turned out to be wrong. You two make a great pair."

"Thanks." I gestured at the rest of the guests who were making their way toward the seats. "And speaking of great pairs, aren't you supposed to be getting married?"

"Yeah..." Shane tugged at his starched collar, "...guess I am."

"You're not nervous, are you?"

He laughed. "This is the third time I've done this. You'd better believe I'm nervous."

"Third time's the charm, right?"

"Damn right."

I followed him over to where everyone was gathering. Eric turned, and the way his eyes lit up, even after he'd seen Shane just a moment ago, I had no doubt the third time was the charm. Didn't even matter that this was the third time. They were perfect together.

I didn't know why they'd chosen this place in particular, but something about it must've meant something to them. Even if it didn't, the view alone made it worth the hike up here.

There were no chairs up here, so the small group of guests stood facing Eric, Shane and the chaplain. As the chaplain opened his Bible, Eric and Shane joined hands.

The chaplain read the ceremony and took them through their vows, and I couldn't help getting choked up. Neither could anyone else, including the two grooms, who were obviously doing their best to keep it together.

Finally, the chaplain closed his Bible and smiled. "You may kiss your groom."

Shane and Eric drew each other in, but paused for a second to exchange grins. Then they kissed tenderly as everyone applauded.

While the photographer had Eric and Shane pose with their families—including both of their ex-wives who'd flown in with their kids for the wedding—Connor and I strolled down to the enclosure below this one. We wandered to one of the lowest levels and stopped beside the chest-high wall, gazing at the scenery below.

"That was a really nice ceremony," I said.

"Yeah," Connor said. "Kind of hard to believe they both would've been kicked out for this a few years ago. Now they've got the base chaplain doing their wedding."

I nodded, running my thumb alongside his hand. "Times are changing."

He looked at me and smiled. "Guess they are."

As we held each other's gazes, his smile faded a bit. So did mine. We shifted our eyes out to the farms and ocean below us. If I had to guess, I'd have bet he was thinking the same thing I was: times were changing, but time was also going by. Quickly. In the military, that meant upheaval and relocation.

There'd been some rumors that I was going to be transferred to another base that was in dire need of an ATO, but both General Bradshaw and Captain Warren had made some phone calls, and at least for the next couple of years, I would remain on Okinawa.

But there were some strings even Bradshaw couldn't pull. In three months, Connor graduated. Once he was no longer a student, he was also no longer a dependent, which meant he'd get booted off the island. Civilian contractor jobs weren't looking terribly promising, and without an income, getting a Japanese visa wasn't happening either.

Connor looked out at the water and sighed. "I'm really going to miss this place."

I chewed the inside of my cheek. "Won't be the same without you."

His shoulders sank, and he winced.

Heart pounding, I said, "I want you to stay."

He laughed bitterly. "I want to stay, but regulations are what they are. I have to go."

"I don't think you understand." I took his hand and squeezed it gently. "I want you to stay. With me."

Connor turned to me, brow furrowed. "I can't. There's no way I can unless we're—" His eyes widened. "Wait..."

I smiled.

His lips parted. "Are you serious?"

Smile broadening, I nodded. "Absolutely." I gestured at the upper level where the rest of the wedding guests still milled around. "Just say the word, and we'll talk to the chaplain."

"The chaplain..." He stared at me incredulously. "You're serious? You...really want to get married?"

Heart racing even faster, I whispered, "Do you?"

Connor swallowed hard. "Not if it's just so I can—"

"It's not just because you're graduating." I let my fingertips drift down his cheek. "I want to. The fact that you're leaving might mean doing it sooner, but I still want to. I've...I've wanted to for a while. I love you, Connor. Even if we were both staying on this island forever, I..." I paused, clearing my throat. "I kind of freaked out in the beginning, but I guess somewhere along the way, I just knew." I ran my fingers through his hair. "I knew I wanted to be with you and nobody else. And that hasn't changed."

He held my gaze, and my heart beat even harder as the silence went on and his expression betrayed nothing.

Cupping his face, I added, "If you don't want—"

Connor laughed and shook his head. "I never said that." He pulled me closer. "You just blew my mind a bit, that's all."

Relief pushed a laugh out of me too, and I wrapped my arms around him. "So is that a yes, no, or maybe?"

His smile said it all, even before he whispered, "It's a yes." He sniffed, and the smile got even bigger. "It's definitely a yes."

I held him tight and struggled to keep my emotions in check.

"I love you," he whispered.

Sniffing sharply, I closed my eyes and held him tighter. "I love you too."

Some voices and movement turned both our heads, and we looked just in time to see the wedding party and the rest of the guests coming down the stairs. We both quickly composed ourselves and, hand in hand, went to join everyone else.

"Hey, hey," I said, grinning as the two grooms came down the steps, also hand in hand. "Congrats again."

"Thanks." Eric beamed at Shane. "I don't think he knows what he's gotten himself into, but..."

"Oh please." Shane laughed. "After all this time, I think I know."

"He *thinks*." Eric gestured at Connor and me. "Well, you two are next. No pressure or anything."

Shane rolled his eyes. "*Eric.*"

"Actually..." I looked at Connor, and we both smiled. I put my arm around his waist and turned to Eric and Shane again. "He's right. We're next."

They both blinked.

"Really?" Eric asked.

"Yep." Connor put his hand on top of mine on his hip. "Guess you guys are a bad influence."

Shane laughed. "When the hell did this happen?"

"About"—I nodded toward the wall where we'd been standing—"two minutes ago."

"Wow." Eric smirked. "He's right. We *are* a bad influence."

"I'll take the blame." Shane winked. "Congrats, guys."

"Thanks." I kissed Connor's cheek. "We'll see you guys at the reception?"

"You'd better be there," Eric said. "We're—damn it, the photographer wants us again."

"Go," I said. "We'll see you guys there."

They left to pose for more photos, and Connor and I slowly made our way out of the castle and down the hill to my car. Near the bottom, Connor stopped.

"So you really do mean it," he said. "You want to make this...permanent."

"Absolutely." I cradled his face and kissed his forehead. "No doubt in my mind I want to do this."

Connor put his arms around my waist. "Where do you think we should do it?" He wrinkled his nose. "Please don't say the base chapel. I hate that place."

I laughed. "No, I was kind of thinking we'd keep it to one of those places where all good things seem to happen."

"Yeah? Where's that?"

"The beach, of course."

About the Author

L.A. Witt is an abnormal M/M romance writer currently living in the glamorous and ultra-futuristic metropolis of Omaha, Nebraska, with her husband, two cats and a disembodied penguin brain that communicates with her telepathically. In addition to writing smut and disturbing the locals, L.A. is said to be working with the US government to perfect a genetic modification that will allow humans to survive indefinitely on Corn Pops and beef jerky. This is all a cover, though, as her primary leisure activity is hunting down her arch nemesis, erotica author Lauren Gallagher, who is also said to be lurking somewhere in Omaha.

Visit L.A.'s website at www.loriawitt.com, her blog at http://gallagherwitt.blogspot.com, and follow her on Twitter where she tweets (usually bantering with Aleksandr Voinov) as @GallagherWitt.

As long as no one asks and they don't tell...

Conduct Unbecoming
© 2012 L.A. Witt

First class petty officer Eric Randall is less than thrilled about taking orders to Okinawa. Three long, lonely years on a crappy island that's thousands of miles from his daughter? Oh. Yeah. Sign him up. But as long as he's stuck here, he might as well make the best of it, so he discreetly checks out the local gay scene.

Shane nearly drops his drink when the gorgeous, cocky-looking guy strolls into Palace Habu. He buys him a drink, and before long, they're making out in a booth. Eric is a straight-to-the-point kind of guy and doesn't want to play games. Since Eric's idea of not playing games is getting the hell out of there and going back to one of their apartments, Shane is more than happy to go along with it.

What starts as a scorching-hot one-night stand leaves both of them wanting more...until Eric finds out Shane doesn't *just* outrank him, he's an officer. DADT may be repealed, but an officer getting involved with an enlisted man falls under conduct unbecoming.

Still, they can't resist their mutual desire. There's no reason anyone has to find out. But secrets have a way of outing themselves.

Warning: Contains two military boys who keep forgetting they're not supposed to be together. Probably because they never have their uniforms on for any length of time...

Available now in ebook and print from Samhain Publishing.

Back from the dead...and back to square one.

No Distance Left to Run
© 2014 L.A. Witt and Aleksandr Voinov

The Distance Between Us, Book 4

The night before Chris and his best friend Joshua were sent thousands of miles apart on their respective Mormon missions, they finally gave in to their mutual desire. Left trying to make sense of what happened, Chris's already shaky faith crumbled altogether a year later, when Joshua suddenly died.

Inconsolable, ostracized by his family and the only community he'd ever known, Chris found his way on his own. Now he's going to school and loves his job as a bartender at Wilde's. Years after Joshua's death, he's finally moving on.

Then a familiar face rocks his world. Joshua isn't dead. He's back in Seattle to make peace with his dying father, with a new name, a new accent...and old feelings for Chris that are alive and well.

Forgiveness doesn't come easy for anyone, but just as Chris is accepting that the man he loves isn't going to run away this time, their families threaten to pull them apart all over again...

Warning: Contains two lost boys who need to make up for a hell of a lot of lost time. There's also a military uniform, a tuxedo, and a knife. In the same scene. And yes, it's that kind of scene.

Available now in ebook and print from Samhain Publishing.

SAMHAIN
PUBLISHING

It's all about the story...

Romance

HORROR

www.samhainpublishing.com

CPSIA information can be obtained at www.ICGtesting.com
Printed in the USA
LVOW07s1043171115

462960LV00004B/199/P